NEW

ORLEANS

BY

GASLIGHT

NEW ORLEANS BY GASLIGHT

VOLUME ONE

EDITED BY BRANDON BLACK

ASSISTANT EDITOR CHRISTOPHER WONG

COVER BY ROBERT CERIO

BLACK TOME BOOKS

NEW ORLEANS, LOUISIANA

BRANDON BLACK AND BLACK TOME BOOKS
ON THE WORLD WIDE WEB:
HTTPS://WWW.BRANDONBLACKONLINE.COM

Acknowledgments

The anthology you are now holding would not have been possible without the assistance of the following individuals: Denise Wong, Christopher Wong, Alan Decker, Cathy Chandler, Robert Cerio, Eva Caye, Deborah Franklin, Michael Scott, Dionne Cherie and David Ducorbier. Special thanks to Chris Smith and the Fiction Writers' Group of the East Bank Jefferson Parish Library where several of the stories herein were critiqued prior to submission. And of course, my thanks to all the authors who submitted short stories and poems for this volume. You're the ones who made this book a success!

Contents

Acknowledgments   4

Brandon Black

- Introduction   7

Philip Karash

- *Welcome to N'Awlins*   10

David Ducorbier

- *ARMS R.A.C.E.*   13

Gary Bourgeois

- *Farewell and Adieu*   33

Robert Cerio

- *Twain, Tesla, and the Ghost of the Old Opera House*   48

Matthew Wilson

- *Steam, Punk*   67

Dionne Cherie

- *Cartoon Whirlwind*   68

Contents

Shawn Aveningo

· *Pocketful of Coppers*   70

Brandon Black

· *Songs of the Divine Pulsation*   72

Jackson Kuhl

· *Crescent City*   105

C. M. Beckett

· *You Gotta Give Good*   117

Jay Wilburn

· *Super Dome*   131

Brandon Black

· *The Gift*   144

Gary Bourgeois

· *Kilkarney's Map*   180

Introduction

by Brandon Black

It is entirely evocative of the city of New Orleans that my father, betrothed to a woman who was not my mother, was stolen away from his fiancée with a sashay and a sideways glance. While ordinarily I could not approve of such a thing, in this case, I reluctantly, if unnecessarily, give my assent, else I would not have been born into this world. Passion flows through this city like the river, an ever-present current that is the life's blood of the city. Whether or not, as has often been said, there is something in the water, or perhaps, in the air, the people of the Big Easy are notoriously of hot blood. In New Orleans, a city seemingly built for the sole purpose of delighting the senses, those who do not have hot blood when they arrive here are assuredly soon to get it.

In this New Orleans That Never Was and Never Will Be, She is both zenith and nadir of Victorian progress – a land of brass-gilded hopes and steel, steam-driven dreams where clockwork carriages and steam-driven streetcars traverse the streets alongside Her fabled carnival floats; and airships, commercial and military, lazily drift overhead like the languid waters of the river below. Only two things are forever constant: the slow, chugging pulse of the river which courses through Her and the amorous passions of Her denizens. Well, three things, if you count the food. The city is a culinary city, utterly synonymous with cuisine: gumbo, red beans and rice, jambalaya, bread pudding, cornbread, fried chicken and biscuits, poboys, crawfish étouffée, king cakes, New Orleans-style mandarin chicken, bananas foster and beignets, for a start. All to be washed down with cafe au lait, iced tea or absinthe as one chooses.

While crime is, of course, an ever-present danger, tales of the city overflowing with vampires are not to be believed as the requisite amount of sin needed to make New Orleans New Orleans simply could not be conducted if there were only the night-time hours to work with.

On Her streets and in Her shops, one will occasionally find a gypsy fortune teller, or a reader of palms and tea leaves. One is free to take her advice or leave it as one wills but it is the wise man who knows never to mock an oracle of the city.

Gambling and prostitution are mainstays of the local economy – both best accompanied with ragtime music. The red light district of Storyville is famed the world over for the nimble skill and inventive perversity of those trafficking their wares. There is no preference, no fetish, no vice, no sin that will not be catered to or indulged in this city where sodomies abound and are practiced as high art.

In the absinthe and opium dens of these fabled Crescent Cities, the gambler, the pickpocket, the con-man, the rabble-rousing politician and the painted whore must all make room at the table for the airshipwright, the clockwork engineer, the giant reptile hunter, the sky smuggler and the air pirate. And although no one saw them enter, and perhaps no one will see them leave, the swamp witch, the houngan and the mambo are seated there as well. These New Orleanses of Nevernever are governed by sultans and padishahs, senators and kings, priests and abbesses, but never absolutely ever by an honest man, for that alone would be unseemly.

New Orleans is a city crowded with whores and charlatans – far too many for them all to find employment in public service. But for all Her faults, She is a beautiful city, an exalted city, filled with wonders and terrors, sorrows and triumphs and both to Her own denizens and to the less fortunate peoples of the rest of the world, She constantly says one thing: that you could do a lot worse.

The city of New Orleans offers all and promises nothing, yielding up neither pity nor compassion for those who fail to find what they seek within – nor for those who find everything they fought, sweated and bled for, yet come to regret.

Cheers,

Brandon Black

Welcome to N'Awlins

by Philip Karash

Arthur didn't know how he had come to be in the shop. The nightly air ferry had dropped him off in the French Quarter, which was obscured by a fog which clung to the street and his skin like the exhaust of an engine. He stumbled through the miasma, disoriented after the lurching journey, and found himself on an old street. Gas fed lamps cast a glare through the mist and revealing a lone door facing him. Candles flickered inside and a sweet smell of spice came from the window. A cafe perhaps? No, a shop of some sort.

As he approached, the black lacquered door creaked open. From the shadows, stepped a lanky man draped in a heavy brown coat. As he donned a battered top hat, he smiled up at Arthur. The light revealed the face of a shrewd man of indeterminable ethnicity, the color of his skin waning from brown to tan in the changing light filtering through the fog.

"Well monsieur, what brings you to my door tonight?"
Arthur, shocked by the directness of the question, did not quite know how to respond."

"I, well...the fog sir. I am new to the city and lost. It was my plan to enjoy some of the entertainment in the Quarter before -"

He was cut off as the man began to circle him, looking him over.

"New to my city? You be needing a guide then?"

"I...I suppose, if you would be kind enough to lead me back. I had planned to take in a show over..."

Arthur looked around for a sign of which direction he had meant to be heading in.

"Where exactly are we, sir?"

A smile, glinting of metal and showing the darkness of some gaps, spread on the face of the stranger as he leaned on a silver headed cane Arthur could not remember being there a moment before.

"You at a Crossroads *mon ami*. You come into the right place. Maybe you looking for *amour*? Or something more powerful? Well, you found it at my shop here. Must remember, N'Orleans be an old city in a new world. We got things happening here from a long time back before people try and change it with gears and steam. City is a living thing. Magic be the blood of her. Maybe I show you some. Show you the real end of the river."

Arthur didn't know what to think. A practitioner of dark arts? Surely a thing couldn't exist...at least not anymore. The world was in the peak of a technological age. Scientists were conquering the skies and seas through the power of steam. Chemical creations once thought to be only capable with alchemy were now available to any boy with a ha'penny.

"Well sir...if you are what you say you are, I could be convinced to take a stroll.

The clockwork cabarets and gambling halls full of Creole sounds could wait. Arthur looked up at the man, but he was already turning into a nearby alley. He slowed enough to give a glance over his shoulder.

"You follow me and I take you to the real city. I show you the things that clockwork can only begin to imitate."

Arthur hurried after him as the mists swirled behind them.

END

Arms R.A.C.E.

by David Ducorbier

The smoke in the room was thick and tears filled his eyes. The billowing clouds impaired his vision to the extent that he closed his eyes and used his hearing to guide him. The sounds of battle and death surrounded him. The sharp report of rifles, the screams of the wounded, the crackle and snapping of burning timbers and thatch roofing. All of these sounds assaulted his senses, yet he knew he had to focus; for somewhere in this maelstrom of horror was the man who was trying to kill him.

As he fruitlessly scanned the room, he tried to recall the layout of the Mission Station. The two-story white washed clay and wood structure contained three barracks halls and an infirmary. It was inside one of the second floor barracks that he had entered via the thatch roof with the other Zulu warriors of his father's *kraal*. He could hear the voices of his fellow warriors in the next room, their battle chants flowing high and low in musical tones. The music was occasionally punctuated by the high pitched screams of the dying, and the harsh barking tones of the white devil's tongue. It was this unmusical sound which alerted him to his enemies' presence. He gripped his *ilkwa* with his calloused hand, the three feet of wood and twelve inches of sharp steel giving him courage. Through the stench of blood and offal, the freshly tanned cowhide on his *isihlangu* steeled his resolve to drive out these

13

foreign invaders.

He slowly moved into the smoke, a slight breeze caused it to swirl. Through the ebb and flow he could see a smudge of scarlet. He swiftly raised his shield, tightened his grip on the spear, shifted his weight to the balls of his feet and leapt into the haze. Halfway through the leap he thrust his spear forward at the spot he thought his enemy might be. He was rewarded with a cry of agony as the sharp steel of his *ilkwa* pierced the yielding flesh of his opponent. In one practiced motion, he removed his spear from the man's torso, only to repeatedly thrust it back into his prone and bloody foe. This repetitive motion with shield and spear cleared the immediate area of the smog that had been hampering his vision.

Looking down he saw the deep crimson of the man's life blood seeping into the bright scarlet of his uniform. The Britannian was a young man with straight brown hair and smooth cheeks which had probably never felt the touch of a barber's razor. He watched as the dying boy's hands frantically searched his pockets, perhaps for some personal or religious item that every Britannian seemed to carry. What he removed looked like a brass egg the size of his fist. Black iron bands encircled the egg and a six inch cylinder sprouted from the top. The boy slid the brass casing off the top revealing a glass tube beneath, inside of which was a luminescent blue crystal suspended within a yellow gel. A small smile played across the boy's lips as he choked out the words "God Save The Queen!", and slammed the glass tube into the egg.

The boy's body went limp and when his hand hit the floor the egg, rolled across the floor to lay gently rocking at the Zulu warrior's feet. Bending down to pick up the strange object, he noticed a sickly green glow begin to emanate from the spot where the tube had been rammed home. Examining

14

the inside, he saw the blue crystal begin to bubble and fizz in the yellow gel which then began to turn green and ooze out the hole and run down the sides. The green rivulets that rolled out were filled with little bubbles which hissed and popped, splashing a tiny amount on his forearm. The pain was immediate and intense.

Dropping the device on the floor, he quickly wiped off the offending liquid on his loincloth.

The egg was now on the floor shaking violently and leaking the green acidic fluid on the wooden planks of the floor which were in turn smoking and melting away. At this point he knew he was dealing with some new infernal weapon created by the Royal Alchemical College of Engineering.

He knew his life was in danger. He frantically searched for the nearest exit to put as much distance between himself and the unknown destructive capability of the latest R.A.C.E. weapon. Broken rays of sunlight streamed through the smoke and shattered makeshift defenses of a window to his left. Without a second thought, he raised his shield and hurled himself from the second story window. The initial blast surrounded him in a cocoon of heat and hurled him thirty feet further than his own momentum had carried him. The secondary blast wrapped him in a cool green mist which reminded him of the cold shallow creeks near his home. As he began his descent to the hard unyielding ground, the cooling effect of the moisture gave way to an agonizing wave of scalding heat. The mist caused his skin to blister and crack, which then changed the color of the vapors from green to red as his blood began to mingle with the moist air around him. The ground suddenly rushed up to meet him.

The impact broke his elbow and slammed his head into the hard packed earth. Blackness swarmed up threatening to swallow him, as golden shapes sparkled and swam through his vision. The loud ringing of bells drowned out the sounds of the explosions which filled the battlefield and surrounding courtyard of the Mission. Through the haze of smoke and his own immense agony, he took in the battlefield in one pain enshrouded glance. The tide seemed to be turning against the Zulu forces. The Britannians had formed up several firing lines and the men behind them were hurling more of those egg shaped creations into the main body of his father's army. The pain of his body was one thing, but the pain in his soul at seeing his father's once mighty *kraal* being decimated by these new technological marvels was another matter entirely. Tears flowed down his face for his father, his brothers in arms, his homeland and his own excruciating pain. He lay there dying and not caring whether he did so or not, when he felt a pair of strong hands pull him into a sitting position. His eyes would not focus and his ears were still ringing, yet he knew those hands. He knew the voice which cut through the fog in his mind which shouted to him.

"My Prince, My PRINCE! We must pull back or we will be ruined! My Prince! You must get up! Get up my Prince!"

"Prince Kwambe. It is time to wake up, my lord. Are you awake sire?" The voice was gentle and warm. It pulled him out of the depths of his nightmare with calm and caring hands. "My prince, it would seem you were having the night terrors again. I thought it best to waken you, lest your cries upset the other passengers." The prince slowly opened his eyes, sat up and stretched his arms and legs before replying. "As in most cases Olwenyo, you are correct. Have we entered the Americans' airspace yet?" Olwenyo was busying himself pulling clothes out of an armoire and placing a bowl of steaming water on the vanity across from the prince's bed.

" I do not know sire, but when I last spoke to the deck steward we were still on schedule. I shall go to the dining level to prepare your meal and inquire as to our exact arrival time. I have laid out your *American* clothes for your meeting with the ambassador." Crossing the rather spacious quarters, Olwenyo gave a slight bow and a nod toward the vanity. "I have also prepared some water if you would like to freshen up before dinner, sir." He quietly slipped out the door to leave the prince alone with his thoughts.

The prince's quarters were large as befit his station. Lifting himself out of the bed with an audible sigh, he made his way over to the vanity to wash the sleep from his eyes. Looking into the mirror, he surveyed the damage of time and war on his face. The heritage of royalty was evident in his strong facial bone structure, smooth skin, and above average height, indicative of access to a better diet than the average Zulu citizen. The deep brown skin color was in stark contrast to his soft green eyes. The tightly woven curls of his black hair were cropped close to his head. The heritage of war was a tableau of horrors written across his entire body, starting from the rough calloused scar tissue which ran from jawline to ear, and down the entirety of his neck, chest and leg, as if a single piece of skin had been flayed from his body. Scars of all shapes and sizes adorned his body like jewelry, rubies of puckered flesh from bullets, thin white diamond sparkled lines from piercing spears, and the crown jewel being the long jagged gash of a sword blade. Looking himself in the mirror, he thought to himself how much he preferred the field of battle than his newest arena, diplomacy. Mentally shrugging, he washed his face and began dressing himself in preparation for a long evening of vapid conversations, absurd compliments, and veiled threats.

Stepping out of his cabin, he adjusted the ruby pin in his light gold cravat and smoothed the front of his navy blue waist-coat. The hallway was empty as he passed the fine mahogany doors of the first class cabins and used

17

the brightly polished brass rails on his descent to the dining level below. The stairwell was carpeted and the walls were papered in a floral pattern, yet the light fixtures were ugly iron monstrosities which spoke to the martial nature of the ships previous life. Upon reaching the next deck, he could feel the vibrations of the airship's mighty twin propellers and the steam engines which powered them in the very soles of his feet. Entering the dining room, he scanned it for any threats, more out of habit than any real danger that might be present. A man in a plain black suit a few tables away from the door stood when Kwambe entered and he beckoned the prince over to his table.

The dining room held ten tables, five per side, each next to a porthole style window so that each table might have a view of the clouds in which they sailed. The prince made his way over to the man. "Good evening Mr. Benjamin. It would seem that this will be our last meal upon the *Gettysburg*. I had hoped to avoid more wasteful talk of how great each of our nations are and how peace is the greatest gift we could give our children. I have grown weary of talking hours on end of everything and nothing at the same time. I find that I much prefer action to words and substance over twaddle. So, for the sake of peace and mutual satisfaction, could we dispense with any more treaty negotiations tonight?"

Judah P. Benjamin was a life long diplomat with curly black hair parted to the side and a boyish face which was accustomed to smiles. Mr. Benjamin's thin eyebrows were raised in shock at these blunt words, yet a smile began to dance across his face. It started in his eyes and then found its way to his lips which began to tremble and then erupt into a large beaming smile. Laughing he replied, "Now this is the man I have been waiting to meet! Would that I could, Mr. Dlobo. I must insist that we speak, but I shall do so with no beguilement or any unnecessary embellishments. Quite simply, the United

18

States government would like to aid you in your endeavors at stopping British colonial expansionism. We are prepared to provide you with material and industrial advisers to help you defend yourselves from the tyranny of Britannia. Yet we can't be seen helping you until after the peace treaty between Zululand and Britannia is signed in New Orleans. Since America can't officially recognize you as a nation, we can't send you any aid. It might be seen as a provocation to war by our allies or the Brits."

Now it was Kwambe's eyebrows which were raised in shock. A look of disbelief and incomprehension was written all over the prince's face, and as he prepared to voice these feelings the American diplomat continued his revelations. "Zululand is filled with great deposits of the newly discovered element *Africannium*, which has unlimited potential in the areas of energy and warfare. Your kingdom's lack of raw materials and manufacturing will be it's downfall. When we arrive in New Orleans, you must make your father realize that in order to remain free, he must embrace change and enter the Age of Steam. Without our aid, you will be crushed under the heel of colonialism and become a puppet state like India."

Finding his voice the prince followed the American's train of thought. "If Britannia gains access to our *Africannium* deposits, they will have found a power that rivals or even surpasses that of steam. Perhaps new weapons and faster forms of transportation which may threaten America in it's currently weakened state." Kwambe reached into his shirt and pulled out a glowing blue crystal wrapped in a leather thong around his neck. Looking off to one side he rubbed the crystal as he said, "Britannia already has powerful new weapons. A month ago R.A.C.E. agents brought them to bear against my people. In time, they will create naval and air forces which would out class anything America or her European allies could put into the field. This would

19

not just be our war. It could very well be the world's war."

After this sobering thought, Mr. Benjamin rallied his thoughts. "It seems you have a gift for theatrics and embellishment that I had not given you credit for, sir. Our reconstruction period is going rather well and believe me when I say that our boys at the Massachusetts Institute of Technology are no slouches. Case in point, we are sitting in a warship converted to commercial use. The *U.A.S. Gettysburg* is one of several dirigibles given new lives in the civilian sector to increase commerce and provide our soldiers with honest labor. No sir, we are doing well. Now once the treaty is signed, we could perhaps sell you some of our surplus airships. Say the *C.A.S. Richmond* perhaps. Just the *Richmond* now, but she can easily be refitted as a fighting vessel with a trained crew."

Kwambe began to see where Mr. Benjamin was heading and tried to cut him off. "I have already taken steps to provide our troops with new weapons, but as you have foreseen they will have to be built here in America due to our lack of facilities. I have a friend in New Orleans which I met while attending the University in Paris. He has created a new weapon which I believe could help us win the war."

Judah pounced on this new information. "I believe you are speaking of our mutual friend Mr. Norbert Rillieux. Norbert and I have had business ventures in the past when I helped him bring his *multiple-effect evaporator* to market. This time, he came to me with a prototype weapon but he had not the means to manufacture more. Upon hearing you had commissioned him for his latest work I thought it in all of our best interests to help him. I have, in fact, built a large number of these new weapons and packaged them for delivery. This has all been done in good faith and in the hopes of fostering a new commercial alliance between our two countries."

Kwambe could hardly believe what he was hearing. This man had given him more information in five minutes than he had heard throughout the entire five day voyage from Africa to America. He didn't know how to respond to these gifts. They were his country's salvation and this man was prepared to give them to him. Trembling, he replied, "What will these gifts cost me?"

Mr. Benjamin raised his hands in a placating gesture. "Mr. Dlobo, our price is reasonable and fair. First of all, let me be clear that I have been the financier of this endeavor and simply wish recompense. That being said, I would also like to be the sole manufacturer of these arms to your country." Leaning in towards the prince he continued. "Now in reference to the needs of America, we only require certain assurances that our aid will be used against the Britannian Empire, and that we will be allowed to purchase *Africannium* from you at discounted prices. We have previously discussed your father's anachronistic attitude. We will also need guarantees that your father will not impede any of the aforementioned points. How did you plan on convincing your father to let you use these "*demonic*" new weapons?"

The prince grimaced as he replied, "I had thought to show him Norbert's weapon when he arrived in New Orleans. I had hoped that a demonstration of its power would be enough to convince him to allow me to build more and bring them home to our warriors. I now see that this was foolish on my part."

Judah nodded in agreement as he said, "It's my opinion that if we circumvent your father and supply him with a victory, he will see past his technophobia. Once he has seen that they are a boon to his forces, he will be more likely to agree to the full industrial mobilization of Zululand. If we could get the weapons to your warriors, are there any generals that you trust to use them in battle?"

21

A feral smile crawled across Kwambe's face. "My battle brother Olwenyo's son is in charge of a force of warriors that has been training in secret with captured Britannian weapons. If we could get them Norbert's weapons we could strike a mighty blow to our enemy. Tell me how we could deliver this gift to my people!"

The American stood up from the table. "As I have said before. The United States cannot help you until there is a treaty in place. That does not mean a private firm with an order placed by you could not deliver your goods. When you arrive at Andrew Jackson Airfield, Mr. Rillieux will be waiting for you. He will have information regarding your shipment and the particulars involved in the delivery. It is my hope that by the time your father's boat arrives, in the next ten days, that we might provide him with a victory. Such a victory might force the Britannia government to sue for peace and allow the U.S. and other European nations to acknowledge your sovereignty." Bowing deeply, Mr. Benjamin's mouth quirked up to one side. "Now I shall honor your request to dine alone. It would seem that you have much to digest."

* * *

Andrew Jackson Airfield was a large square manicured patch of earth with four two hundred foot tall mooring towers at each corner. The airfield was flanked by the newly created Pontalba Embassies, twin block long red brick four story structures, which housed diplomats from across the globe. The riverside was a hub of commerce with both river and foot traffic. The centerpiece was the St. Louis Cathedral, and its neighbors the Cabildo and Presbytere.

This was the view that Kwambe was admiring from the window in the Zululand embassy when he heard a knock at the door. The door opened and Olwenyo ushered Mr. Norbert Rillieux into the suite. Norbert Rillieux was

22

a creole man with skin the color of heavily creamed coffee. His wavy black hair was parted down the middle and he wore a loose fitting tan sack coat.

Kwambe made his way over to Norbert and embraced him like a brother. "I'm glad you are here. Now that we are in private, we may discuss the delivery of your inventions to my warriors." Norbert glanced to the corner of the room where a tall ebony skinned man with a muscular physique stood eating small green strips of sugar cane. Kwambe followed Norbert's gaze. "Pardon me Norbert. That is General Mala and you need not worry. He is the head of security for our embassy. Please continue."

Norbert shrugged, "Well, I have secured transport for the weapons on the airship *Anubis*. Her captain is a Liberian who is known as *The Jackal*."

The prince looked disturbed as he said, "Isn't this man a well known air pirate!"

Norbert calmly replied, "He prefers the term privateer, but yes he is. He has been called the *Scourge of the Clouds* by more than a few governments. That being said, he is also known to be an honest businessman who asks few questions, and the *Anubis* is the fastest airship on this side of the Atlantic."

Seeing that the prince was content with his answer he pushed on. "We must go to the public air docks at the end of Decatur Street with our final payment. Once he has been paid, he should have the weapons in your warrior's hands in three days."

Kwambe was startled by the speed of the delivery estimation and could barely contain himself. The prince began to make his way to the door, "Let us go without delay! Olwenyo has already secured the payment and awaits us downstairs."

General Mala stepped out of his corner, "Your Highness, give me time to assemble the guards, that we might accompany you. The Decatur street

23

docks are well known for their unsavory characters."

Kwambe dismissed the general. "We must move quickly and I do not wish to attract any undue attention. Thank you for your concern. Come Norbert, we shall go give this *Jackal* of yours his payment." Seeing the look of disgust on the generals face, Kwambe turned to Norbert. "Perhaps on our return we could have another demonstration of your weapons power for General Mala's benefit."

Mr. Rillieux nodded agreement and followed the prince out of the suite. General Mala made his way over to the window and watched Norbert, Olwenyo, and the prince make their way to Decatur street. Turning, he strode out of the room, leaving a tiny pile of little green stalks on the floor next to the window.

The three men made their way down Decatur Street heading to the public air docks across the street from the French Market. Making their way to the market, Kwambe was taken aback by the sights, sounds, and smells that surrounded him. Men and women were hawking their wares, vendors and customers loudly haggled over prices, the smell of exotic foods and spices mingled with the pungent odor of the unwashed masses. Winding through the maze of vendors' stalls in the French Market, one particular stall drew the prince's attention. The man behind the wooden trestle table was an old pale white man with liver spots dotting his bald head. He wore a collarless white shirt with a long leather apron. He had a tarnished silver monocle on his left eye and was engrossed in his work. He was examining a flintlock style pistol with brass ringlets, vacuum tubes sprouting from the sides and a glass orb in its center. The table was covered in an array of firearms ranging from tiny guns that fit in the palm of your hand, to large two-handed behemoths requiring shoulder straps.

Kwambe leaned over to examine the man's current project. "What sort of weapon have you created there, my good man?"

The aged tinkerer examined the well dressed African hovering above him. If he were upset at being addressed by a black man his tone gave no indication. "I wish that I had created this marvel. I am only replacing a burnt out vacuum tube. This is the *W.B. Befuddler.*"

Kwambe replied, "What a strange name. I presume that it is named after its inventor."

The tinker gave the prince a curious look. "You mustn't be from here, and by here, I mean America. It's named after its inventor and its first victim. The W.B. stands for Wilkes Booth and the Befuddler comes from President Lincoln. It's said that the President was asked how he felt after being shot and he replied '*befuddled*'." Chuckling, the oldster finished his narrative. "The great emancipator even granted freedom to his would be assassin in exchange for the schematics of the weapon and a promise to stick to acting in the future."

Norbert edged closer to Kwambe to keep his words private. "Your Highness, we mustn't be late for our appointment. I also believe Olwenyo is getting nervous holding a carpetbag full of money as well."

Grudgingly, the prince consented.

The old man's ears perked up at the words "highness" and "money" and quickly introduced himself. "The name is Henry Eckers the Third. If I may be of any service to you, please come see me. I am here everyday selling and repairing all manner of weaponry."

Reaching into his pocket the prince produced a Morgan silver dollar and pressed it into the tinkers hand. "This is for your illuminating tale. Perhaps I will have more time to examine your goods another day."

The old man stammered his thanks as the three men exited the market and crossed the street to the public air docks.

Henry stared in awe at the well-dressed black man who had just given him a week's pay for a story that every American knew. Before he returned his attention to his work, he noticed four unsavory looking men peel off a nearby wall and follow the prince. Hatred boiled in the men's eyes as they shadowed the trio. The old man twisted a new vacuum tube into the *Befuddler* and looked over to his apprentice dozing in a chair behind him. "I'll be right back. If anyone even touches my merchandise, shoot 'em!" Tucking the gun into his apron, he turned and went after his newly adopted benefactor.

The air docks were a flurry of activity. Dockworkers and sailors bustled from ship to shore loading and unloading cargo from around the world. Norbert walked confidently down the docks. He passed rows of mooring masts and gangways, until he came upon a most decrepit looking dirigible. It was a simple air bladder, filled with hydrogen, surrounded by a huge cargo net which secured it to the airship. The vessel itself had been a seagoing galleon in its previous life and still had barnacles clinging to her hull. The only parts of the ship that didn't belong to the turn of the previous century were the engines. The four fifty foot long brass cylinders attached to two steam engines provided the *Anubis* with her forward thrust and her reputation for speed.

Several shirtless men of various races prowled the decks and climbed across the cargo netting securing provisions for the long journey to Africa. Norbert stopped at the gangplank leading to the airship and hailed a nearby sailor. "Ahoy there!" I'm looking for the Captain. Tell him we have his money."

A red haired man with sunburnt skin acknowledged Norbert and went below deck.

Kwambe grimaced, "Ahoy there?"

Norbert smiled, "I've always wanted to say that."

The prince was preparing his reply when he saw four burly men making their way over to them. The men were dressed in shabby clothes and were caked in filth with bushy unkempt beards. The man in the lead of this band was wearing a threadbare grey coat with yellow piping on his sleeves and gold epaulets on his shoulders. Once they were within twenty feet of the prince, the grey coat looked over to one of his confederates. "Now what do we got here Clem? Look at these fancy niggers!" This statement was greeted with raucous laughter by the grey coat's troops.

The man referred to as Clem replied, "I think they stole your bag Colonel. Didn't you just say some negro ran off with all your worldly possessions? I'll be damned if that don't look just like your carpetbag."

The Colonel's mouth opened into a large smile which revealed a set of perfect white teeth. Olwenyo clutched the property in question close to his chest as he looked to the prince for instruction.

The Colonel was the first to respond to Olwenyo's actions. "Now looky here boys. Why don't you just hand over that there bag and we'll just let you go with a warning. If you decide to put up a fight, well then, I can't be held responsible for what might befall you bloody negroes."

Norbert drew himself up in a pugilist's stance and filled his voice with a bravado he did not feel. "I must warn you! I am trained in the arts of self defense!" The white men burst into laughter at the sight of Norbert's defiance.

Kwambe used the distraction to issue Olwenyo his orders in their native tongue. "The only thing that matters is getting the captain his money and our warriors their guns. You must get on board the vessel and beg the captain to lift off. I will handle these mongrels. Now GO!"

27

Olwenyo looked him in the eyes and after a small nod he bolted up the gangway. The white men screamed in rage as their quarry fled onto the airship. The Colonel calmly voiced his opinion. "Now that was a mistake boy." Norbert was still watching Olwenyo's hasty retreat when his world was sent spinning from the impact of a fist smashing into the side of his face. The blow knocked him to the ground and his assailant pounced on top of him and continued to pummel him about his face and body.

Kwambe planted his feet and raised his fists as two of the men flanked him to either side and the Colonel came straight at him. The one called Clem came at him from the right with a wide hay-maker. Kwambe stepped into the blow, and blocking it with his left arm drove his right fist into Clem's throat. The strike knocked Clem to his knees and he gasped for breath while clutching his throat. The prince knew an attack would be coming from his rear and threw a wild punch in that direction to ward off the other attacker. The swing served its purpose and the other man was forced to dodge backwards to avoid his fist. The Colonel and his companion began to circle Kwambe as Clem lay on the ground wheezing. They danced around each other as they searched for a weakness in one another's defenses. Kwambe found an opening, and as he prepared to strike, he felt Clem's hands wrap around his ankle and jerk him to the ground. This caused the prince to instinctively put his hands down to brace for the fall. This was the opening the Colonel had been looking for as he barked his orders. "Billy! Restrain him!"

Kwambe was fighting to maintain his balance when Billy pounced on him and locked his arm behind his back. The prince struggled to free himself but his arm was firmly pinned against his shoulder blades. Clem struggled to his feet and then proceeded to brutalize the prince's face as the Colonel watched the action with a detached and professional calm.

28

Meanwhile, Norbert was putting up the only defense he truly knew, which was to roll upon the ground kicking and screaming for help. Looking through a haze of blood and tears, he saw his foe stand up and pull a knife from his boot. Norbert redoubled his cries for assistance and was rewarded by a feeble shout from the tinkerer they had just met in the market.

"Leave that man alone!" The knife wielding man whipped around and was suddenly surrounded in a crackling blue corona of energy. Norbert's assailant shook violently and fell to the ground in a twisted twitching heap.

The Colonel heard the discharge of the *Befuddler*. Turning to look, he saw his man lying on the ground and Henry moving to help Norbert. "Clem. John is down. Would you be so kind as to escort that elderly gentleman to the gates of Hell!" Clem's fist delivered another vicious blow which was accompanied by a sickening crunch. Looking down at his handiwork, he saw that he had broken the prince's nose with his last punch. Nodding to the Colonel, he acknowledged his orders and raced to intercept Henry. Closing the distance between them, Clem saw the oldster raise the pistol and pull the trigger. Nothing happened. In the final steps before Clem reached him, Henry was feverishly slapping the gun in his palm and screaming obscenities. Clem snatched the gun from Norbert's rescuer and backhanded him across the face. Norbert tried to stand and defend the old man, only to be rewarded with a swift kick to the ribs.

Satisfied that Clem had the situation under control, the Colonel turned his attention back to Kwambe. "I told you not to put up a fight. Now we'll probably have to kill you." Kwambe mentally assessed the damage to his body. His nose was broken, his left eye was beginning to swell shut, his lip was split, and his tongue was pushing against a loose tooth. Looking up at the Colonel, he tried to speak as clearly as his battered face would allow. "You

29

were going to kill us anyway. R.A.C.E. agents never leave witnesses."

The Colonel didn't even pretend to be shocked by the allegations. "What gave us away? I will need to rectify those errors in the future."

Blood was still pouring from the prince's nose and lip as he smiled in response. "Go fuck a hyena! I will not aid you in bettering your inadequate skills of subterfuge, you pig-faced son of a whore!"

The Colonel smiled as he replied, "This is why the Crown installs puppets as heads of state. They are much more polite. With you dead and your father soon to follow, we will pick a warlord who will be suitably gracious. A man who will sign a peace treaty with my country and allow us to fold it into our bosom. So that we may keep its resources safe from envious neighbors who would steal your people's birthright. Well that's what we told them. Your army has a surprising number of dissatisfied generals in it. One in particular was very helpful though. He called a council of war in your father's absence. Your father's *kraal* will be camped and leaderless in the valley of Isandlwana when Britannia's army sweeps in and massacres them." The Colonel produced a Bowie knife from under his jacket. Pulling the blade from its sheath he turned it over a few times to allow the sun to gleam off its sharp edge. The colonel drew back the knife as he prepared to thrust it into the prince. "Goodbye Mr. Dlobo."

Kwambe raised his head and locked eyes with the Colonel. The crown prince of Zululand was determined to meet death honorably as a proud Zulu warrior. Suddenly a scream shattered the moment. "KWA-ZULU!" A bolt of green fire sizzled above Kwambe's head to burst into the chest of the Colonel. The Colonel's lifeless body tumbled back as his limp hands dropped the knife which fell clattering on the cobblestones at Kwambe's knees. The prince seized the knife and rammed the point under Billy's chin and drove it

30

deep into his skull. The pressure on Kwambe's arm ceased immediately and the prince slumped to the ground.

Clem turned from a battered Norbert to look in horror at what had befallen his comrades. Standing there at the prow of the *Anubis* stood Olwenyo cradling a heavily modified Springfield rifle. Its long five foot form was cased in brass with rivets dotting the length of the barrel. Above the rifle stock was a two foot long glass cylinder filled with a viscous yellow fluid. Black tubing ran from the cylinder into a detachable magazine in front of the trigger guard which cast a pale blue light. The sight of this intimidating weapon and the destruction it had wrought on his commanding officer broke Clem's spirit. He ran down the nearest alley to escape as Olwenyo began to take aim at him.

Norbert and Henry slowly limped over to Kwambe and helped him to his feet. Kwambe looked at Henry with the eye that wasn't swollen shut. "Mr. Eckers, you have a warrior's spirit."

Henry's pale skin began to redden from the compliment. "It wasn't nothin'. Kinda wish I had a warrior's body to go along with it. I know you must be hurtin' real bad sir, but people round here don't take too kindly to black folk killin' white folk. Self defense or not, I think it would be best if we got outta here."

Norbert nodded vigorously as he responded. "I can testify to that your Highness. I think we should retreat to the embassy and give this a few days to blow over. It should be safe by the time your father arrives and the treaty negotiations begin in earnest."

Olwenyo called down to Kwambe. "Sire, wait for me. I'll be right down!"

Kwambe waved him off. "No. Your duty no longer lies here. You must ensure that your son gets those weapons and goes directly to Isandlwana.

General Nthanda is a highly respected warrior that the men will follow. He must get the *kraal* out of Isandlwana before the Britannia arrive. The army must be saved or we will be forced to capitulate. We would have to sign a peace treaty that would make death preferable! Now go! Tell the Jackal to take off before the authorities arrive!"

Olwenyo raised his rifle in salute and dashed below deck to inform the Captain of the situation.

Kwambe put his arm around Norbert's shoulders and let him carry his weight. "Let's go Norbert. I have a bottle of rum from the Haitian ambassador with our name on it. Mr. Eckers, I would be pleased if you could join us for a drink."

Henry rubbed his bruised cheek. "I think a drink sounds mighty fine, your Highness."

The men moved quickly to a nearby alleyway as the crowd of onlookers began to grow. Kwambe allowed himself to be helped by both men now that the adrenalin of combat had begun to wear off. His head drooped on his chest as they navigated their way down the alley. In the dim light, just before he drifted off into unconsciousness, he thought it was odd to see a small pile of green sugar cane stalks in the gutters.

END

Farewell and Adieu

by Gary Bourgeois

Chauvin began singing in a ragged baritone, "Farewell and adieu to you, Spanish Ladies …"

"Will you stop?" Lemoyne hissed in a low voice. "What's the matter with you?" Short, plump, and conniving, Lemoyne twisted around on the donkey cart's seat. He turned his head from side to side to see if Chauvin's singing had awakened anyone and brought them to their windows. Satisfied that everything remained quiet among the dark, shuttered, brick cottages on either side of the narrow street, he turned on his companion in the cart.

"Have you forgotten what we're doing is against the law? If we're caught, we'll be flogged, thrown in jail, and then flogged again."

"I'm sorry. This one just set me to singing is all," Chauvin replied. Chauvin was tall and broad and more suited for physical than cerebral labor.

"Well, stop it. There'll be time to sing later, after we're paid. You sing better when you're drunk, anyway." Lemoyne snapped the reins over the donkey's back, urging the animal to quicken his pace over the wet, uneven paving stones. "Or, maybe, you sound better when I'm drunk. Anyway, just be quiet, we're almost there," Lemoyne said, inclining his head toward the lighted windows in the four-story-tall brick tower two blocks away.

The Observatory, as most people in New Orleans knew the tower and its adjoining home, was the subject of a great deal of speculation in the city. Its builder and occupant, Professor Charles Möbius, proclaimed a strong interest in astronomy when explaining his unusual nocturnal activities. But rumors were spreading, fueled by purchases of strange chemicals and exotic herbs and by the clandestine visits of unsavory characters like Lemoyne and Chauvin, that there was something sinister taking place at night within the tall, ominous brick tower.

Lemoyne maneuvered the donkey cart around to the rear of the tower, where the back entrance was hidden from view. He hopped off the cart, took one last look around, and knocked on the heavy wooden door. He had to knock several times before he heard the locking bar being withdrawn from the inside.

No matter how many times he saw the professor's misshapen, hunchbacked servant, the initial sight of Iago always made Lemoyne winch. Besides his crooked spine and the large hump behind his right shoulder, the left side of Iago's face drooped disturbingly, slurring his speech. The eye on that side of his face was milky white and bulgy.

"Oh, it's you," Iago said when he opened the door. "What do you want, Lemoyne?"

"I've got a package for the professor. Tell him it's a fresh one, no more than a few hours old."

Iago grunted then shuffled to the side to see past Lemoyne to the bundle in the back of the cart. "All right, bring it in. I'll get my master."

* * *

Chauvin carefully set the bundle down on a large, wooden table in the first floor room of the tower. There were no interior walls and no floor. Cobwebs festooned the underside of the heavily timbered second story floor

34

above their heads. The rough table was the only article of furniture. Abandoned jars, beakers, and vials, many cracked and broken, littered the dirt floor around dusty stacks of crates and boxes. A steam engine sat against the inner curve of the brick wall. Flames flickered in the engine's firebox to the accompaniment of the soft hiss of escaping steam. A single oil lamp, suspended over the table, was the room's only source of light.

Presently, Professor Möbius – greying, portly, and dressed in a purple, silk smoking jacket–came down the stairs that led to the second floor. He was followed by Iago.

"Well, Mr. Lemoyne, Iago tells me you may have something for me tonight."

"That's right, Professor. This one's special, no more than a few hours old. I brought it over directly I got my hands on it."

"Well, then, let's have a look, shall we?" Möbius walked to the head of the table and untied the cords holding the bundle closed. He unfolded two layers of coarse cloth and revealed the sunken, death-pallid features of a young, dark-haired woman. "Do you know the cause of death?" Möbius asked, leaning over to examine the corpse's face.

"Died of the bloody flux, I was told."

Möbius pinched the cheeks and pulled open the lid of one darkly circled eye. "Yes," he said. "There are signs of dehydration, but the tissue is still quite malleable and the eyes relatively clear."

"Like I said, Professor, this one's special, died just this afternoon, hasn't even been planted yet. I got it right from Charity Hospital morgue, had to pay a pretty picayune to an orderly to let me take it out," Lemoyne said. "So, there'll be a bit of an extra cost, you see."

"No one to be missed, I trust?" asked Möbius.

35

"Oh, no, Professor. No visitors in the hospital, no family, no friends, on the way to Paupers' Field."

"I think she's Spanish," Chauvin offered, then grimaced as the professor slid his hand under the cloth and began squeezing his way down the young woman's upper arms and torso.

"Yes, it's in excellent condition. Quite easily the best specimen you've brought me, Mr. Lemoyne. I'm very pleased. I think, Iago, I will try my latest batch of elixir tonight." Möbius' eyes gleamed in anticipation. "Success has eluded me, Iago, but tonight I feel it within my grasp. Take the subject upstairs."

"Yes, master." Iago picked up the woman's corpse and placed it over his right shoulder.

"Her name is Ángelita," Chauvin said.

"You didn't tell me you knew this one," said Lemoyne, surprise and annoyance evident in his tone.

"Oh, I don't," said Chauvin. He reached into a pocket and took out a chain and medallion. "Her name is on the back of her little holy metal." Suddenly uncomfortable with two and half pairs of eyes on him, Chauvin added, "Well … I just wanted … a little something … and I didn't think anyone would be missing it."

Möbius raised his eyebrows. "Yes, to be sure." He counted out some silver coins from his pocket and handed them to Lemoyne. "This, I think, should cover your expenses, and the cost of your efforts in transporting the specimen here."

"Oh, yes, sir, Professor, this will do nicely. If ever I get hold of another one as fresh, I'll be sure to bring it right over."

"By the way, Mr. Lemoyne, would you and your associate be

interested in making a little extra money tonight?"

"Would you be needing another body, sir?" asked Lemoyne.

"No, actually I need a bit of help operating the steam engine."

"Ah, well, thing is, I'm not much on technology, Professor," Lemoyne answered.

"It's not that complicated, Mr. Lemoyne. I'm sure even you can catch on to what I need done. If you'll step over here, please, I shall show you."

Iago trundled the cadaver up the stairs while Lemoyne and Chauvin followed Möbius to the steam engine.

"The problem," Möbius said, "is the relief valve is stuck and won't open at its appropriate set point. Which means the boiler could over pressurize and explode."

"That would be bad, right?" Lemoyne asked, taking off his hat and scratching his head.

"Oh, yes, very bad." Möbius pointed to a gauge mounted on the engine's boiler. "This is the pressure gauge. The needle indicates the pressure inside the boiler. If the needle goes into the red area here, it means the pressure is too high and it must be relieved manually by opening this valve. Once the pressure has dropped into the safe area, the valve can be closed, like this." Möbius closed the valve and the hiss of venting steam ceased. The gauge's needle started to slowly rise. "I will need the needle to stay in the upper register of the gauge for the success of my experiment. Now, Mr. Lemoyne, if you would, put a couple more shovelfuls of coal into the firebox."

Not inclined to physical labor Lemoyne turned to Chauvin. "You heard the man, put some more coal on the fire."

"More coal means a hotter fire and a hotter fire means more steam and more pressure," Möbius explained as the needle steadily rose. "Once I divert the steam to the piston, the pressure will drop, but should start to rise again as the new coal is consumed. All you and your associate will have to do, Mr. Lemoyne, is watch the needle. When it gets close to the red area, open the valve. When the pressure goes down, shut the valve."

"That's easy enough, then," said Lemoyne.

"If the pressure should drop below the halfway point on the gauge, then just shovel in some more coal. Now, then, Mr. Lemoyne, why don't you do the honors? Open this lever here and start the engine."

A delighted grin spread over Lemoyne's face as he gripped the lever. "Look at me, I'm an engineer!"

Chauvin laughed and imitated the sound of a steam whistle. "Woo-woooo!"

"Yes, to be sure," Möbius commented with a dry smile.

Lemoyne opened the lever and the steam engine's piston began to move. Lemoyne and Chauvin watched captivated as the piston's up and down motion was transmitted by the engine's machinery to a large, circular pulley. The wide leather strap around the pulley began to move, as well. The strap ran up through a square opening in the floor above.

Professor Möbius had to yank on Lemoyne's arm to get his attention. Raising his voice and speaking directly into Lemoyne's ear to be heard over the noise of the engine, he said, "Remember, Mr. Lemoyne, watch the needle on the gauge."

* * *

The young woman's corpse, clad only in a dingy hospital gown, lay on a wooden table on the second floor of the tower. As on the first floor, the second floor had no interior walls. Oil lamps, hung on chains from the underside of tower's lofty roof, ringed the space above the table. A smaller oil

38

lamp, mounted on the brick wall across the floor, illuminated the area around an electrical generator. Beyond these circles of smoky light, the second floor of the tower was wreathed in shadow and darkness.

Möbius had inserted steel needles into the dead woman's disease-thinned arms. One needle was draining her blood from a vein into a ceramic crock on the floor. The other needle, connected to a hand pump, was introducing into an artery a pinkish fluid from a large, glass jar suspended over the table. The glass jar was labeled *Elixir of Life, batch XXIII.*

As he worked the hand pump Iago sang in a bass voice slurred by his deformed face.

"Someone's in the kitchen with Dinah.

Someone's in the kitchen I know.

Someone's in the kitchen with Dinah,

Strummin' on the ol' banjo."

Möbius, wearing a surgeon's gown and cloth cap, puttered about constantly. He checked the flow of blood into the crock, the progress of the elixir in the glass jar, the condition of the tissue at the cadaver's extremities, and then back to a side table to consult his notes. All the while muttering to himself. "Yes, yes. All goes well, very well, indeed."

When Möbius saw the pinkish elixir being expelled into the crock, he called out, "Iago, stop. The Elixir of Life now fills the veins." Iago shuffled out of the way as Möbius excitedly disconnected the rubber tubing from the needles in the woman's arms. "The electrodes, Iago, quickly. And remember, positive goes to the right arm and negative to the left. Or is it … no, I said it correctly the first time."

Professor Möbius carefully attached the electrodes to the steel needles in the corpse's veins. Stepping back, he said in an awed voice, "Now,

Iago, engage the generator."

"Yes, master."

"Iago, wait! Don't forget your goggles. We don't want anything to happen to your eyes. Well ...to your eye."

"Yes, master." Iago fumbled with his goggles, trying to fit them to his misshapen face. When he had gotten them into as reasonable a position as possible, he scuttled across the floor to the generator.

Grabbing a large handle with both hands, Iago heaved and levered the steam engine's leather drive belt from the idler onto the generator's pulley. He hopped back as a surge of electrical energy pulsed from the generator and sparked and popped along wall-mounted cables to a rusted and dented electrical box. The box was mounted on the brick wall near the table upon which the corpse lay.

Möbius watched the needle on the box's voltmeter spike into the desired range. "Yes, oh, yes," he said, his voice rising in excitement. Wisps of acrid smoke rose from electrical box's interior. Eyes gaping wide behind the lenses of his goggles, Möbius grasped the handle of the double-bladed electrical switch screwed into the tower's brick wall. "Now, Iago, now I restore life to where it once has fled!"

* * *

"What do you think he's doing up there?" Chauvin stood at the foot of the stairs that led up to the second floor. "You don't think he's one of them, do you? That likes dead girls for... well, you know." Ever since Lemoyne's attempted explanation of necrophilia a couple of years ago, Chauvin had generally stopped asking questions about their clientele's intentions.

Lemoyne was seated on top of the wooden table, away from the deafening clamor of the steam engine. He was cleaning under his fingernails with a folding knife. "What, the professor? Nah, all them bodies we been bringing him, he's trying to bring them back to life."

"Really?"

"Oh, sure. You know them jars of blood we bring him from the undertaker's? Well, he mixes chemicals and the like into that to make up these elixirs of his. The professor thinks once he gets the right combination of chemicals, he'll be able to bring the dead back to life."

"Do you think he'll be able to bring Ángelita back to life?"

"Nah. It ain't possible. Once you're dead, you're dead. And that's the end of it."

"What, don't you believe in heaven?"

"Me? Nah, heaven's just a fairy story the priests tell to get people's money. Just another rafters' racket, it is. But mind you, I wouldn't mind having a piece of that action."

Chauvin, an expression of deep uncertainty on his face, turned away from Lemoyne and looked up the stairs. "Still, I'd like to see her if the professor does bring her back." He laid his hand on the banister and started up for the second floor, the wooden stairs creaking under his weight.

Lemoyne watched Chauvin climb the first few steps and then with a shrug, went back to cleaning his fingernails, whistling *Camptown Air Race*.

* * *

With a dramatic flourish Professor Möbius closed the switch. A powerful electric current coursed through the lifeless body on the table. The corpse jerked and shuddered. The eyes opened and closed asynchronously. Legs kicked erratically. Hands and fingers beat wildly upon the tabletop. The chest convulsed spasmodically, as if fighting for one labored breath. Then the

41

body arched, supported only by the back of the head and the heels, and, astoundingly, the mouth flew open emitting a prolonged, piercing scream of primal pain.

Have I achieved success? Has new life been created? As these thoughts registered in his fevered mind, Möbius hurriedly opened the switch, cutting off the flow of electricity through the young woman's body.

The body flopped back on the wooden tabletop. And lay still.

Slowly, warily, Möbius approached.

* * *

Lemoyne finished scraping the dirt from under his fingernails. He folded the knife and put it back in his pocket. He looked at the stairs for a while and then at the steam engine. Curiosity had gotten the better of him, but he had a responsibility to discharge.

Sliding off the table he walked to the boiler and checked the gauge; the needle was just above the halfway mark. It was with some distaste that he looked at the shovel in the coal bin, but he spat into his hands and took it up. He used the blade of the shovel to unlatch and open the door of the boiler's firebox. Taking a shovelful of coal, Lemoyne tossed it onto the fire and watched with satisfaction as the flames flared up.

Well, he thought, *there's no telling how long it will take to attempt to raise the dead.* He threw in a second and then a third shovelful. Just to be on the safe side.

* * *

The body on the table lay still. Eyes open, staring – sightlessly? – into the darkness beneath the tower's high ceiling. Möbius stood close by, searching anxiously for any sign of life – a slight flaring of the nostrils, the minutest rise or fall of the chest, a dilation or contraction of the pupils – anything that

42

would prove his experiment a success.

He had just begun to reach for the wrist to feel for a pulse, when the eyes blinked.

"Iago. Iago, it lives," Möbius said in a voice hushed by the wonder of his achievement. "It really lives."

"You've done it, master," Iago said, joining Möbius at the side of the table. "You've given her life."

With a suddenness that made Möbius and Iago step back, Ángelita sat up. She looked around puzzled, as if seeing the world for the first time. Ignoring the two men, she seemed more interested in her surroundings.

Möbius stepped forward and addressed her. "I am Professor Charles Möbius. You are my creation, the culmination of decades of research and experimentation."

Ángelita twisted around to look behind her.

Möbius cleared his throat and addressed her again. "I am Charles Möbius. I gave you life."

Ángelita looked down at her hands and feet. She wiggled her toes.

Möbius tried again, this time in a softer tone. "My child, I am your father."

"Her name is Ángelita, master," Iago prompted.

"What? Oh yes, her name. Angelina, I am …"

"No, master, it's Ángelita."

"What?"

"Ángelita, master."

"Iago, this is very important, please, try and enunciate."

Iago rolled his eye. "Án-ge-li-ta."

"Yes, you see, Iago, that was much better. Ángelita, …"

43

Ángelita responded immediately to the sound of her name. She looked directly at Professor Möbius, her head cocked at an angle, as a puppy might.

"Oh, yes, that's more like it. You are a clever child. Ángelita, I am Da-Da."

"'Thou know'st 'tis common,'" Ángelita said in an accomplished, theatrical voice. "'All that lives must die, passing through nature to eternity.'"

"Er … I beg your pardon?" Möbius asked.

"'To die – to sleep,'" Ángelita continued, her ashen-grey face underscoring the subtle inflexions of her words. "'No more; and, by a sleep to say we end the heart-ache and the thousand natural shocks that flesh is heir to, 'tis a consummation devoutly to be wished.'"

"Isn't that …?" Iago asked, letting his voice trail off.

"Shakespeare? Yes. *Hamlet,* I believe," Möbius answered.

"Well," said Iago. "I wouldn't have expected this."

"'If I must die,'" Ángelita intoned with passion. "'I will encounter darkness as a bride, and hug it in mine arms.'"

"Oh, I like that one," said Iago.

"Which play is it from, though? Let me think … Ah, yes, I have it, *Measure for Measure,*" Möbius said, a note of triumph in his voice.

"'Of all the wonders that I yet have heard,'" pronounced Ángelita. "'It seems to me most strange that men should fear; seeing that death, a necessary end, will come when it will come.'"

"*Richard III?*" guessed Iago.

"Oh, no, that's from *Julius Caesar,*" Möbius admonished. "What on earth made you say *Richard III?*"

Iago shrugged his deformed shoulders. "Just a hunch."

44

Lemoyne found Chauvin on the second floor near the top of the stairs. "So, what's going on?" he asked. "What's the professor been up to?" When Chauvin didn't answer Lemoyne looked under the circle of lamp lights. And there, plain as life, sat Ángelita. "Well, I'll be damned," he said. "The old bugger actually did it."

Chauvin, however, did not hear him.

He had reached the top of the stairs as Ángelita had flopped around on the tabletop like a fish out of water. And he had seen the miraculous moment when she had sat up and begun to speak – to speak in such a way as he had never heard. Chauvin liked music and song, but he had never heard words spoken before as music. As music the way Ángelita spoke them. He walked forward, drawn to her voice, drawn to her.

Ángelita, seeing Chauvin approach, said, "'Eyes, look your last!'" She raised her arms to him. "'Arms, take your last embrace!'"

Chauvin took the medal and chain from his pocket and placed them in her outstretched palm. "Miss Ángelita," he said. "I'm sorry I took your little holy medal. I didn't mean nothing by it."

She closed her fingers around the chain and with her free hand grasped Chauvin's shirt front. "'And lips, oh you the doors of breath, seal with a righteous kiss,'" she pulled his lips to hers, "'a dateless bargain to engrossing death.'"

Ángelita slumped back upon the table, the chain and medal dangling from her dead hand.

Chauvin, still feeling the soft pressure of her kiss, put trembling fingers to his lips.

Professor Möbius was mildly surprised to find Lemoyne standing beside him. "Mr. Lemoyne, that last jar of blood you brought me ..."

"Yeah," Lemoyne responded to uncompleted question. "I think it was from an actor what died last week sometime."

"Ah," said Möbius. "That may explain some of what has occurred here tonight." Several moments ticked by before he added. "By the way, Mr. Lemoyne, who is watching the boiler?"

"Aw, you don't need to worry, Professor," Lemoyne said. "I put lots of coal on the fire before I came up."

From below, on the first floor, Professor Möbius heard the unmistakable, low-pitched groan of metal being stressed beyond its limit of endurance. "Oh, dear," was all he had time to say.

* * *

The explosion of the boiler – besides waking up nearly everyone in the city – had blown a hole through the brick wall of the tower and had destroyed half of the second floor. All four men and the donkey had survived. Along with some relatively minor steam-burns, the men had suffered various lacerations and contusions, but no broken bones.

Professor Möbius had explained the presence of the dead woman to the police by claiming she was a recently hired domestic who had become curious about his nightly experiments. Apparently, as he had told the police, she had awakened from her normally peaceful slumber, had entered the tower to see what was going on, and, quite tragically, had been killed when the boiler exploded. The police, busy with other matters, had asked no further questions. To add credence to his story, Möbius purchased a wall vault in St. Louis Cemetery under the name Ángelita Montague.

Ángelita was laid to rest on a cool, but bright, fall morning. A tired priest, accompanied by a bored altar boy, muttered mechanically and hurriedly

46

through her graveside service.

After the priest and altar boy left Chauvin pulled a nearly empty bottle of rum from his coat pocket. He took a full swallow and handed the bottle to Iago. "I feel better now," Chauvin said, "knowing she has a place with a name on it."

Iago wiped his mouth and chin on his sleeve and handed the bottle back.

Chauvin took another drink. "Do you believe in heaven?" he asked.

"Oh, yes," said Iago smiling. "I believe in a heaven where I will have a straight, healthy body and no master save God."

Chauvin nodded. "I believe in heaven, too." He finished off the remaining rum and slid the empty bottle back into his pocket. He then began to sing in a clear, resonant baritone.

"Farewell and adieu to you, Spanish Ladies,

Farewell and adieu to you, Ladies of Spain;

We'll drink and be jolly and drown melancholy,

And we hope maybe someday to see you again."

When he had finished singing Chauvin touched his fingertips to his lips, and smiled, a single tear rolling down his cheek.

END

Twain, Tesla, and the
Ghost of the Old Opera House

by Robert Cerio

Sam Clemens inhaled deeply, drawing the acrid cigar smoke into his mouth and rolling it around his tongue. He had purchased it from a tobacconist on Decatur street that had hand rolled it that morning, but it still lacked the sweet tang of a hand rolled Havana. He cursed himself inwardly for not packing another box of them in his steamer trunk for his trip, but there was have been no way for him to know he would be away from home this long, or that his layover in New Orleans would have to have be extended for as long as it had been. As he sat on the edge of the Toulouse street wharf, he imagined that there were worse places to have to stay on for a week or two. For all the Crescent City lacked in cigar options, there were still plenty of delights to be found here that rivaled the best European cities.

He looked down at the telegraph in his hand that he had received two days ago, and checked for the name of the steamer he was waiting for. Looking at the river, he could see the Steamer *War Eagle* come around the bend at Algiers point, looking to the world like a stately birthday cake whose candles had been dipped in pitch. He stood and walked over to the slip as the *War Eagle* pulled in, and her deck crew set about tying the massive ship to the wharf.

As the deckhands lowered the ship's long stages into place, the local stevedores began unloading huge bales of cotton and luggage. One of the deck crew noticed Sam waiting patiently at the end of the gangway as the passengers began to disembark amid the growing chaos that often accompanied the arrival of a large ship.

"Mister Twain!" The dark skinned deckhand exclaimed, giving him a curt salute, "It's good to see you again."

"Relax before you sprain something, son." Sam said with a grin, "I haven't held rank on a ship for over thirty years."

"Yes sir." The young man said, "Are you here to see Captain Ransom?"

"Ransom is still in command of the old girl?" Sam said with some surprise, "I would have thought he would have died with a pickled liver a long time ago."

"His new bride is a teetotaler." The deckhand said, "Made him give up the drink almost five years ago."

"Amazing." Sam said, looking down the ramp as passengers passed the two of them, "But I'm not here to see your skipper. I'm waiting on one of your passengers. An old friend."

"Oh! The scientist fellow!" The deckhand said with recognition, "He had mentioned he was meeting a writer friend. I didn't realize he meant you, sir."

"Well, there are a lot of writers that call New Orleans home these days, so there was really no reason to assume, lad."

49

"That friend of yours is an odd one, Mr. Twain." The deckhand said, "He gave the men in the cargo hold no end of difficulty about how they handled his crate. Insisted that it was full of very delicate equipment."

"It probably is." Sam said, "It isn't often that I've known Mr. Tesla to travel without a lab full of equipment."

"What on earth for?" the deckhand asked.

"For when inspiration strikes!" said a short man with a thick European accent behind them.

Sam turned to see his friend Nikola Tesla, standing on the dock, pulling a dolly with a large crate on it behind him.

"I should have known that you would have come ashore with your equipment." Sam said, greeting his friend with a warm handshake, "How have you been, Nik?"

"I have been well." Tesla said, "Of course, I had to have them switch my cabin. They put me in cabin number five initially."

"The horror." Sam said sarcastically, "Did they move you to six?"

"Nine." Tesla said.

"What was wrong with Cabin 5?" The deckhand asked.

Tesla looked at the man like a zookeeper would look at a particularly obnoxious chimp. "It wasn't divisible by three, of course."

The deckhand looked at Sam in confusion. "Never question a scientist about the nature of the universe, son. It will only make your head hurt."

The deckhand walked away looking even more confused and went about his duties.

"So, my friend... I got your cable and came as soon as I could. Now would you please explain why you've pulled me away from my work?" Tesla asked, "I certainly hope that this isn't one of yours and Livy's plots to set me up with yet another woman."

"I wouldn't dream of it." Sam said, "Livy hasn't given up on you yet, but I am quite content that you will forever remain a bachelor. You're here at the request of an old friend of mine, Walter Flower."

"The Mayor?"

"That's right." Sam said flagging down a carriage, "He was just a reporter with the Picayune when I worked the docks here. We paid our dues together cobbling together pieces for his bear of an editor."

"So, what's the problem?" Tesla asked.

"Well..." Sam said pensively. Tesla had known the man for years, and knew that it was unusual for him to be at a loss for words.

"Come on, Sam..." Tesla said, "Spit it out."

"Apparently, the city has a ghost problem. The Mayor asked if I would look into it."

"A ghost problem."

"That's right."

"You brought me fifteen hundred miles to check for monsters under the mayor's bed?"

"I would think you would know me better than that. I've talked to a few people while waiting for your arrival, and there's something damn peculiar going on at the Opera House." Sam said, climbing into the carriage as the driver carefully loaded Tesla's crate onto the roof of the buggy.

"I saw this play the last time I was in Paris." Tesla said, "Is there a disfigured but charismatic genius involved?"

"You're way too hard on yourself Nik." Sam said with a smile, "You may not be the best looking man in the world, but I wouldn't call you disfigured."

"Funny." Nik said with a frown, "So tell me about this 'spirit'. Is there liquor involved?"

"Only if we're lucky." Sam said, instructing the driver to take them to their hotel on Royal Street to drop off Tesla's luggage and equipment. After Sam assured the eccentric scientist that he had made sure his room number was divisible by three, They walked the block over to the opera house on Bourbon street.

The last rays of light were still catching the top of the huge facade of the opera house, lighting it up like a fiery beacon even as the shadows gathered on the street below. The local bars, cafes, and music clubs slowly began to stagger to life around them. Tesla looked carefully at the cafe on the corner, observing young couples drinking coffee with an aristocratic air even as American sailors staggered past them in a drunken search for loose Creole women. A faded sign on the side of the tall building announced that "Les Huguenots" would be performed here in just a few days.

"As I understand it the ghost starts out here and makes its way down the street, wailing with sorrow until she disappears." Sam said.

"Wailing with sorrow." Tesla said, "And you base this on..."

"Research." Sam said proudly, "I looked into the history of the apparition in question. Supposedly, it's the ghost of a woman looking to avenge herself upon a lover that spurned her."

"Sam, Let's get something straight right now. It's not a ghost." Tesla said with authority.

"I don't know, my friend." Sam said, "Witnesses describe her as having long white hair, blood red eyes, and glowing a ghostly shade of purple."

"Glowing, you say?"

"That's right. You have to admit, Nik... it certainly sounds like a ghost."

"Sam, I can make a globe glow from across the room by filling it with the right gas and applying an electric current. Does that mean I've somehow captured a spirit?"

"Well, no..." Sam said, pulling out another cigar, "But it's always sent a chill up my spine."

"That 'chill' is nothing more than static electricity." Tesla said. "We should go inside. Did the mayor provide you with a key?"

"He did." Sam said, "I'll wait for you by that door."

"Thank you." Tesla said, "I won't be long."

In the years that Sam had known Tesla, he had come to accept many of the quirks that made the man a genius. One of the more annoying of these quirks was that Tesla felt compelled to circle the block three times before entering any building. Sam wasn't sure, but he believed it had something to do with the particular brand of superstitious nonsense that Nikola was exposed to in the small Croatian town he grew up in. Sam was almost done with his cigar by the third time his friend came down the street. He carefully put it out on the wall next to the door and dropped it at his feet.

The large door opened with a deep sounding groan as the two men entered the darkened lobby of the opera house. In the waning light, the deep reds of the velvet curtains and benches that adorned the room reminded Sam of a San Francisco bordello he had once found himself in after a particularly interesting book signing. Their shoes clacked loudly on the marble floor as Tesla looked around carefully at the walls and ceiling.

"Interesting Mural." He said, looking up. Sam saw that he was looking at the intricate angels that frolicked in the painted clouds above the

53

room.

"I suppose." Sam said. The room was getting darker, and he reached for a nearby candelabra. "It's a comforting image if you believe that sort of thing is what awaits you on the other side. Me, I feel I'll be lucky if Satan uses a slightly duller pitchfork."

"Tell me about your research." Tesla said, stooping down by one of the huge windows to examine the edge of a curtain, "Exactly who do they believe this ghost of theirs to be?"

"The locals I spoke to called her Marguerite." Sam said, pulling a box of matches from his pocket, "She's known as the 'witch of the opera'. Her house stood right here before it was demolished to build the opera house. Supposedly, she committed suicide because her lover cheated on her with a younger woman. In her suicide note she vowed that she would come back to exact revenge upon the lad in question."

"I see." Tesla said, "It was nice of her to warn the boy. These witnesses you spoke to, did they say what she was wearing?"

"Not much, from what they told me." Sam said lighting the candles, "She is said to be naked apart from what appears to be a bedsheet. I suppose the afterlife would be appointed with linens."

"Hmm." Tesla said frowning, "You would think a stark naked woman walking down the infamous Bourbon street would arouse more interest from the local constables. Sam, could you bring that light over here?"

"Sure." Twain replied, crossing the room to where Tesla was crouched down, "The ghost keeps extremely late hours, according to those that have seen her. Even the police have to sleep sometime."

"Not in New York." Tesla said pulling a small glass tube and brush from his pocket, "You were there the night they burst into the lab at one in the morning."

"To be fair, that harmonic resonance device you were working on was shaking the whole block." Sam said, "It was probably the neighbors that summoned them after you vibrated them right out of their beds. Say, what have you got there?"

"I'm not sure." Tesla said, scraping a white substance off of the curtains and into the glass tube. "At first I thought it was Talc, but it seems to have a stickiness to it. Residue of your ghost passing through this window, if I'm not mistaken."

"Residue?" Sam said, "You mean ectoplasm?"

"More likely greasepaint, I should think." Tesla said, examining the glass tube carefully, "We are in a theater, Sam. It's far more likely that your apparition is simply a woman."

"But what about the glow?" Sam pointed out, "That can't be done with greasepaint."

"True enough... but as I circled the block, I realized that this window alone cannot be seen from the main street." Tesla said standing up and brushing himself off, "If one wanted to make an appearance as if from 'the ether' this would be the spot to do it from. As far as the glow, that french woman... Curie, I believe her name is... she's been experimenting with a few luminescent materials for some time now."

"Just like a woman to use science to make better makeup." Sam said with a snort.

"Oh, I doubt that." Tesla said, "The last paper I read on her work suggested that the isotopes in question could be quite dangerous with prolonged exposure."

"Women risk much in the name of fashion, my friend." Sam said,

"You can't tell me that those ten inch stiletto heels those girls in Storyville wear aren't a risk to life and limb."

"Regardless, I've been working on a device to detect decaying isotopes." Tesla said, heading for the door, "If that is how your phantom glows, we may be able to track it."

"What on earth would you need such a device for, Nik?"

"Do you remember a few years ago I tried to take a photograph of you, using a Geissler tube for lighting?"

"I remember it not working." Sam said, "All that showed up on the film was the lens screw."

"Right. Well, since then, I've been conferring with a German scientist named Roentgen. I believe that there was a form of radiation involved called an X-ray, that actually looked right through the solid matter."

"That's amazing, Nik." Sam said impressed, "The applications of such a device would be staggering."

"The problem is, I believe there are side effects." Tesla said, opening the door. "During one experiment with such a device, I burned myself quite badly."

"So you developed a device to detect these rays and materials that produce them as a precaution?"

"Precisely." Tesla said, "And the device is back at the hotel."

It took them a couple of hours to return to the hotel and find the device in Tesla's huge crate of equipment. It was bulkier than Sam had imagined it would be, and had leather straps to wear it on one's back. The thing was mostly wood and brass, with large readout dials attached to a sensor wand at the end of a long cable. Tesla insisted that Sam be the one to wear the thing, as he was in better shape despite the ten year difference in their ages.

"You know, the last time you strapped me into one of your gadgets it gave me the runs." Twain reminded his friend as he adjusted the straps. Tesla's "Invigorator" machine produced low frequency vibrations that caused the subject to feel a rush of vitality. When Sam had offered to be a test subject for his friend, he was also among the first to find out the machine's drawback of liquifying the bowels.

"Pheh." Tesla snorted, "The most this one will give you is a bad rash."

"Funny." Sam said, "I feel ridiculous, Nik."

"But you look great. Just like a real scientist." Tesla said, pulling the glass tube from his pocket. The needle on the gauge in Sam's hand didn't budge as Tesla waved his sample under the wand.

"Are you sure it's on?" Sam asked sarcastically.

"Positive." Tesla said, "We just need a larger sample to calibrate it."

The pair made their way through the gaslit French Quarter back to the Opera House. The condensation of the night's humidity gave the cobblestones beneath their feet an unearthly glow in the flickering lights. On Bourbon street, a few of the bars and coffeehouses were still open, but the lively crowd from earlier had dissipated considerably.

"We'll have to go back inside." Tesla said as they approached the old Opera House, "There was more of that greasepaint on the curtain, but we'll have to get closer than outside to calibrate the detector."

"Fine... I'll just wait here looking like a damn exterminator. Just hurry up and get your three loops of the block out of your system."

Tesla gave him a quick, comical salute and jogged down to the next corner. Sam sighed and pulled out another of the inferior cigars, carefully snipping the end while juggling the detector's wand in the crook of his elbow.

57

He lit it and let the smoke fill his mouth and sinuses. Not a Havana, he thought... but it would do. The stagnant humid air of the New Orleans night mixed with the unfamiliar flavor of the cigar as Tesla made his first pass.

"You know those things will kill you someday?" Tesla jibbed him as he jogged past.

"So will overexertion from strange, obsessive compulsions." Sam laughed as his friend rounded the next corner again.

The street had gotten strangely quiet. In the distance Sam could hear the steady clopping of horseshoes on cobblestones. He was tapping the ashes off of his cigar on the wall of the building when he heard the unearthly howl.

"What in blazes?" He said aloud to himself. He poked his head around the corner of the now closed cafe, and the sight that greeted him was one that flushed what little color that remained from his hair on the spot.

From the alley a ghostly, glowing woman appeared, wrapped only in what looked like a bedsheet. Her flowing white hair was matted, and draped around her shoulders, damp from her tears. She was glowing a bright bluish-purple, and her eyes were a vicious shade of red. Her mournful wail cut through Sam like he had been lanced through the heart with a hot poker. She turned to Sam with a demonic look in her eyes.

His cigar dropped from his lips still lit, sending up a flutter of red cinders as it struck the pavement.

"Mother of God..." Sam said quietly as he found himself backing away involuntarily. The apparition turned from him and began strolling slowly down Bourbon Street, wailing in sadness and terror as it went, disturbing the remaining drunks and night owls as she passed them. Most ran, and Sam was about to do the same when he was suddenly grabbed from behind.

Tesla spun his friend around to face him. "Did you calibrate it?"

The famous writer just stared at his friend, mouth agape. "Snap out of it, Sam!" Tesla said as he slapped Sam in the face, "Did you calibrate it?"

Clemens shook his head, and placed a hand to his cheek where Tesla had hit him. "That was uncalled for."

"So, no." Tesla said, grabbing Sam by the wrist and pulling him after the ghost, which was already about to round the next corner.

The pair raced down the block, knocking over a startled drunk that chose that moment to stumble out into the street to see what the commotion was about. Sam started to help the man to his feet, only to be yanked forcibly away by Tesla. Ahead of them, the apparition rounded the next corner less than twenty yards away.

Tesla sprinted ahead as Sam tried to keep up the pace. Though in excellent shape for his age, the weight of the backpack was slowing him down considerably. He rounded the corner at least three seconds after Tesla had, only to find the quirky scientist cursing at the empty air in his native Hungarian tongue.

"Where did it go?" Sam asked between breaths, leaning heavily on the corner lamppost.

"Quickly, give me the calibration wand." Tesla said. Sam handed him the device, and Tesla swept the air in front of him fervently. He looked at the gauges mounted to the wooden handle and frowned. "Impossible. Not a quiver of the needle."

"Impossible?" Sam asked, "How so?"

"Nothing could glow like that thing was and not give off some form of energy, Sam." Tesla said, sweeping the ground with the wand.

"And it was definitely glowing." Sam said still catching his breath, "I also noticed that it seems to have disappeared into thin air!"

"Look around us, Sam." Tesla said waving his arms around, "There are at least twenty places on this street a person could have ducked into in the amount of time I lost sight of it. Damn it man, what happened to you back there?"

"I apologize that the supernatural is a little outside my experience." Sam said, "I just didn't think the damned thing was real until I saw it. I figured we'd turn up some fool in a Mardi Gras costume."

"I'm still not convinced we haven't." Tesla said, "This could still just be some kind of elaborate parlor trick."

"But it was glowing a bright purple, Nik!" Sam said, "That's not something you can do with mirrors!"

The scientist furrowed his brow, pondering for a moment. "Not with mirrors..." Tesla said, scanning the nearby rooftops with his eyes, "But with reflected light."

"A spotlight of some kind?" Sam asked, "But any spotlight I've seen would have illuminated the entire street as well, Nik."

"Perhaps." Tesla said, making a quick calculation in his mind, "If it was a projection of some kind it would have to be from a rooftop that has a direct line of sight to this entire stretch of street."

Sam began scanning the rooftops overlooking Bourbon street, and could see that only one of the old Spanish style buildings fit Tesla's description. As the pair approached the carriageway to 624 Bourbon street, Sam paused for a moment.

"Nik... this is a private residence, and it's awfully late." he said to his friend, "Maybe we should wait until morning?"

"If whoever lives here is involved with our 'ghost', I'm sure they'll be awake."

Sam grabbed Tesla's hand before he could pound on the door. "Maybe... but we certainly don't want to be waking the neighbors as well. Sound carries down these carriageways you know. Trust a southern gentleman on this one. You pound on that door and you'll likely wake everyone whose home is attached to the courtyard."

Tesla frowned at him. "Very well." He said, "but we are still going to have a look around, if it doesn't offend your southern sensibilities."

"Fine." Sam agreed, "Let's just try to be quiet about it, okay?"

"Sam, If I didn't know better I would swear you were scared." Tesla said, "Surely you saw worse than a crying woman in the war..."

"The damned thing rattled me, I admit." Sam said, "It's the thought of a tortured soul wandering the earth for eternity that really gives me the willies. I'm not sure I want to know if it turns out to be real."

The pair made their way down the carriageway and into the silent courtyard. Sam looked around for a lit window, but the courtyard was dark except for a flickering gaslight in the center. He was about to suggest that perhaps they should wait till morning to continue their investigation when Tesla tapped him roughly on the shoulder. Behind a trellis on the back of the building, there was a large industrial cable that seemed to lead all the way up to the roof of the house.

"How on earth did you see this?" Sam whispered at his friend.

"It's humming." Tesla replied, "Just like the coils in my New York lab. It's an extremely low frequency, but certainly doesn't belong in a New Orleans courtyard."

Tesla tested the trellis to make sure it would hold his weight, and began to climb. Sam removed the bulky backpack from his shoulders and considered for a moment that they would surely be mistaken for prowlers if any of the homeowners awoke at that moment. His curiosity somehow banished the thought as he followed his friend up the trellis, trying not to look down. Tesla helped him onto the pitched roof, where someone had mounted a spotlight.

Tesla walked over and threw a small brass switch on the side of the light, which began to hum loudly enough that even Sam could now hear it, but it did not light.

"Doesn't seem to work." Sam said, "Bad bulb perhaps?"

"I don't think so." Tesla said, swinging the spotlight around to face Sam. The writer's white linen suit began to glow brightly in the night, startling Sam enough that he had to fight to keep his balance on the roof.

"What in blazes?" Sam exclaimed, "What the hell is that thing, Nik?"

"I believe it's a Wood's lamp." Tesla said, "There's a professor in Massachusetts, Robert Wood, that has been experimenting with lamps that emit light outside the visible spectrum. He's been working on using it as a form of long range secret communication, but someone has obviously adapted his technique here to make ordinary white objects glow."

"But why?" Sam asked, "To what end other than to scare unsuspecting New Orleanians?"

"I suspect those answers lie at the other end of this cable." Tesla said, turning off the device.

The climb down the trellis was much easier for Sam than the climb up. They followed the cable across the courtyard and into the rear of an abandoned theater that faced the side street. The cable snaked through a doorway that was conspicuously free of cobwebs, and was hooked up to several batteries and a large steam powered generator. A faint glimmer of candlelight peeked under a nearby door that led to the main stage, barely

62

illuminating the room enough for Tesla to inspect the equipment.

"Very clever." Tesla remarked, "Using the batteries keeps anyone from noticing that the generator is powering their ghostly effect."

The men both turned when they heard what sounded like women laughing beyond the stage door. Quietly, Sam crossed the room, and pushed the door open a crack so that he could see what was going on upon the stage.

Several women in dark purple robes were gathered on the stage in the flickering candlelight, surrounding a woman dressed entirely in white. From her height and long hair, Sam was reasonably certain that the girl in the center was their ghost. He waved Tesla over to the door and did his best to listen in to the conversation taking place.

"Sister Marie St. Laurent," One of the women whose face he could not see began, "You have honored our dear departed Marguerite, and in doing so have proven yourself worthy of the Mystic Order of Les Mysteriouses. Do you pledge never to reveal the nature of our organization to any man, be he constable, priest, or lover?"

"I do." Sister Marie said.

"Then welcome to the Krewe." The other woman said.

Sam decided at that moment that he had heard enough, and swung the door open, his sudden appearance making the women on the stage jump.

"Do you mean to tell me that scaring the bejesus out of me was all for some damned initiation?" Sam said with fury in his voice, "Why, I have a mind to report you all for creating a public panic, and let your husbands take you out behind the woodshed!"

Tesla came up behind him. "I don't understand, Sam..."

"It's a Mardi Gras Krewe." Sam said, not taking his eyes off the robed women, "Creoles do love their secret traditions, but this goes beyond

63

good taste. Your secrets will be on the front page of the Picayune tomorrow Ladies, and that will be the end of this ghostly nonsense."

One of the women approached him slowly, removing her hood. As the pale orange light illuminated her face, Sam was surprised to realize that he knew her. Amanda Flower, the Mayor's wife, gazed at him with her dark green eyes.

"Mr. Twain, certainly we can come to some sort of arrangement." she said without a hint of fear in her voice, "I apologize if we upset you."

"Upset me?" Sam said, trying to contain himself, "I nearly soiled myself!"

"And for that, we are truly sorry." Mrs. Flower said, "We wanted your credibility, but not at the expense of your dignity."

"Sam's involvement with this was no accident, was it?" Tesla asked, before Sam could bring forth a litany of curses, "He was part of your plan, wasn't he? To convince the locals that there really was a ghost."

"Very astute, Mr. Tesla." She said.

"But to what end?" Sam asked, trying to contain his growing outrage.

"The hope was to convince my husband and his political friends that the ghost of Marguerite was one that needed appeasement, by allowing us to have our all-women Mardi Gras Krewe operating openly." She said, "It had the added bonus of being a good test of our initiates like Marie here."

"By parading down Bourbon street in only a bedsheet and makeup." Sam said sarcastically, "Wonderful plan, ladies."

"Actually, Sam..." Tesla interjected, "As plans go, it wasn't a bad one. Obviously the Mayor believed in it enough to want an objective outsider like yourself to look into it."

"With a little prodding from his wife, no doubt." Sam said with a

64

glare.

"But think about it for a moment." Tesla said, "If this ghost of theirs gets the credibility of a famous author behind it, the city fathers then have to act or face public outrage. One of their wives suggests appeasing the ghoul, and it works. The women get their Krewe, and the ghost suddenly stops appearing. Rather devious actually."

"Thank you Mr. Tesla." Amanda said proudly.

"Stop taking their side, Nik!" Sam said angrily, "Of all the manipulative, conniving..."

"So says one of the greatest pranksters I know." Tesla said, cutting him off with a bemused glare, "Come now, Sam... if it had been me to be so startled and not you, you would be having a good laugh at my expense right now."

Sam glared at Tesla, but calmed considerably upon seeing the bemusement in the scientist's face. "I suppose I would." he said with a sigh.

"Then you'll keep our secret?" Amanda asked.

"We will." Sam said, "But I hope you ladies will understand that there is no way I will put my journalistic credibility on the line for this nonsense Find yourselves another dupe."

"Absolutely." Mrs. Flower said, "Thank you, Mr. Twain."

The two men left the theater the way they had came, leaving the women to their business. As they made their way back to Bourbon street, Tesla could see the dejected look on his friend's face.

"You alright, Sam?" he asked.

"I would write the whole thing up and sell it as fiction if it didn't make me look like such a fool." Sam said, "Well... that is if I hadn't just promised not to."

"Come on, Sam. I'll buy you a drink." Tesla said, "Mother always said, 'when a woman makes a fool of you, there's always liquor'. Of course, it loses something in the translation..."

"Mother Tesla was a wise woman." Sam said, following his friend into the nearest open bar.

END

Steam, Punk

by Matthew Wilson

Men with money talk hot air.
But still the water runs out.
Since factories filled the air with smog.
New Orleans has been a city in the sky.
Elevated on massive machines
to keep its civilians breathing.
Higher than the yellow clouds.
But now the water is running dry.
And the great machines are straining to
support its crumbing foundations.
Peddle faster, son. We must all do our part.
Till the rains come and give us water.
To fuel the machines, and grind their gears.
The cogs whistle like angry kettles,
but men on peddle bikes generate the power.
And blow the cartilage from their knees.
Peddle faster for we need the steam, punk.
Soon the rains will save us.
And New Orleans shall claim the clouds.

END

Cartoon Whirlwind

by Dionne Cherie

for Jade

* * *

Slink coordinates through the gawking lass

toward a spoken tale you embellish

with ravens and knaves and riddles

after garbanzo salad and tea leftover from the party

as you follow the breeze to holes

in plywood shielding open windows

making animal shadows on the doubled pane.

Even garbed in the coolest shorts and hat

and armed with a fan and wire hangers

I cannot channel the forecast

since March hopped the tracks to October

dealing us this heat post Gustav.

Carrollton Avenue draws like a pen name for Dodgson

where the hardware store is

lame as the gas spent to find generators out of stock.

I shall be late to bolt an axe where the rafters crease

should that surge chase Segnet through Avondale.

My lip is white with the taste of seeing

the black-and-beige etched velvet chairs

and inlayed Cheshire table likely sentenced

to molding in the lagomorphic pool of August.

END

Pocketful of Coppers

by Shawn Aveningo

Puffing on the pipe of cherry tobacco,
lifted from the chest pocket
of an unsuspecting suitor,
Colette tries to form smoke rings
in the shape of a heart.

Regardless the city or the era,
demand never in short supply
for a quick fuck from a lass
laden in leather corsetry.
Eager for a man
to grind her like the gears
of a perpetual time machine,
she liked the way he left
fingerprints of soot down her spine,
and a pocketful of coppers
on the bureau.

She's unable to discern this balcony
from any other Bourbon Street hotel,
as her palms grip the wrought-iron banister,
tightly, mimicking her taut cunt.

Another afternoon spent
collecting coins,
like she collected men
to pay the rent.

Mesmerized by a steam dirigible
floating through a dusty amber sky,
she remembers it's hurricane season,
and bites into a caramel praline.

END

Songs of the Divine Pulsation

A tale of steampunk erotica

by Brandon Black

Free City of New Orleans,
1821

Having scaled the wall facing away from the cobblestone street, the one with the fewest and smallest windows, Vespers then sought to descend from the roof of the château to one of the large windows at the front of the building. The street was quiet and deserted, and the only light other than the stars themselves were the tiny flickerings of little gaslights up and down the boulevard. Vespers engaged the galvanic battery and the little winch at her waist began to lower her slowly via a cable from the rooftop towards her target. Having reached her destination, she disengaged the capacitor and slid a small flattened piece of metal between the gap in the two large window panes and neatly flipped the latch over. Vespers was pleased the device was working so well given that Evan had cobbled it together from spare parts they had found. She smiled to herself in the night-time silence; despite his skill as a tinker, Evan would be very cross with her to know she had trusted her life to something he'd built from junk. From a pocket on a bandolier, Vespers produced a small can of oil with which she oiled the hinges of the window before opening it. It slid silently into the night and stepping upon the windowsill and disengaging herself from the cable, Vespers crept into the large, ornate house, her features wordlessly beaming a smile both of conquest and anticipation.

Vespers delicately alighted upon the floor of the mansion and surveyed the dark room. It was deserted, save for herself. The door leading to the rest of the house was closed. Around the room were many fine objets d'art that would fetch a good price on the black markets of the city: silver candle holders, fine paintings, a silver tea pot and strange, ornately carved ivory statuettes of figures Vespers couldn't place. It hardly mattered. Silver and ivory were things she could sell. Vespers pulled a canvas bag out from a leather pouch and crept towards the candle holders and the statuary.

A woman's voice rang out. "Stop."

Vespers froze and as she tried to turn her head towards the sound of the woman's voice, found she could not. She was completely paralyzed; it was as though she had lost control of her body. Her stomach churned and she felt fear rising up from her belly but try as she might, she could not move.

From out of the corner of her eye and into her full field of vision slowly walked a woman who seemingly coalesced out of the living darkness itself, clad in a full-length linen chemise, purple in color, a beautiful woman with a heart shaped face, long, flowing hair and striking, piercing eyes.

"I am Sabine, and this is my château. You should tell me why I shouldn't have you killed and if I were you, I'd be very convincing about it." This last the woman spoke with a tone that spoke more of boredom than anger. Wooden heels tapped slowly across the floor as the woman withdrew from Vespers' field of vision back in the direction she had heard the strange

73

woman speak from before. Vespers screamed – or rather, tried to. Not a sound left her throat.

"Please don't try that again," Sabine said. "It's not that anyone would hear you – or that anyone would come if they did. It's just that I find the sound distressing." Heels slowly tapped their way against the floor again. There was the sound of someone being seated on leather cushions and then the woman spoke again. "You are free to move."

Vespers whirled in place to see Sabine seated on a leather chair near the fireplace. Vespers would have sworn, did swear, the room was empty. Even in the darkened room, there was no way she could have missed someone sitting there. Yet, there she was. And then there was the matter of the inexplicable control this woman seemed to have over Vespers' own body.

"I said you should tell me why I shouldn't have you killed," Sabine repeated.

Vespers swallowed. "Look – I'm just a thief. I didn't mean you any harm. I just wanted to – "

Sabine cut her off. "You just wanted to rob me. Yes, I understand that part. But still – why should you walk out of this room alive?"

Vespers did her best to seem calm. "You can't just kill me. Just call the Sheriff and he'll come and take me to jail."

Sabine barely but perceptibly shook her head. "I have no interest in the authorities and they won't come here in any case. I've seen to that. You'll have to do better."

Sweat began to bead on Vespers' face. "It's because they won't come here that I picked this place," Vespers lied. "People talk. You don't get many visitors, the Sheriff and his men avoid even coming down this street. I can help you – I can tell you how to make the house more secure – you need better locks on the windows..."

Sabine waved her hand in the girl's direction. "Enough." She poured herself some tea from the pot, the beautifully decorated one Vespers had been eyeing so voraciously, added sugar and milk to the contents of a fine white china cup and sipped delicately. Then she rose from her chair and walked over to Vespers. Vespers tried to turn and dive for the cable dangling by the window but found she could not move again.

Sabine stood before Vespers, looking her over very carefully from head to toe and then extended her index finger outwards towards Vespers' forehead. All Vespers could do was close her eyes. She could feel the very sharp tip of Sabine's fingernail against the skin of her forehead – the trickle of a single drop of blood as it flowed down her face – and – something *else*. There was a moment of dizziness, like she was going to lose her balance, which was another impossibility. Vespers ran the rooftops of this city. They were hers. She *never* got dizzy but somehow, in this place, she felt like she was almost about to faint.

Vespers opened her eyes to see Sabine standing before her with all the gleaming delight of a cat who'd swallowed a canary. "Perhaps your life has some value to me, after all."

* * *

Evan, a young man of African-American descent, made his way through the New Orleans marketplace clad in a white shirt and brown trousers held up with suspenders. On his head was a bowler with his goggles set on the brim and around his waist was his tool belt, which he largely went nowhere without. Evan went through the parts and clockwork mechanisms available for sale in the Gaulish Market, doing his best not to draw attention to his true purpose: lifting wallets and pocket watches from unsuspecting travelers. The

75

guise of being a tinker was not entirely a falsehood though, as Evan did have quite a hands-on knowledge of clockworks and he aspired to one day put those skills to use for his daily bread. Evan snacked on a small bag of peanuts he had obtained in the market and decided to make another round through the crowd before leaving.

The nuts scattered across the floor of the open air market as the bag slipped from Evan's hand. Zoe, that's got to be Zoe, he thought, looking at the girl whose face he recognized but seemed yet strangely different from the girl he knew, including, for a reason unknown to him, a strange, asymmetric hairdo. Instead of its familiar brown, her hair had been dyed completely black. Vespers' hair was nearly shoulder-length on one side but just past her ear on the other and on the short side she had a single braid of hair hanging down over her face decorated with multi-colored glass beads. She looked like the girl he remembered but not. He narrowed his eyes peering at that all too familiar face. It was her, he thought, it was Zoe. His heart leapt in his chest – *She's alive*!

"ZOE – ZOE!! IT'S ME!! ZOE – CAN YOU HEAR ME!?" Evan shouted over the crowd.

Vespers looked around until she looked in his direction. Evan jumped up and down and waved his arm and could see she had spotted him when he saw her smile. She made her way over to him and raced into his arms for a hug.

"Oh my God, Zoe – I thought you were dead. I – I just knew you'd gotten yourself caught and that you were dead," Evan said with tears in his eyes.

Vespers teared up herself seeing Evan getting so emotional. "I did get myself caught, but I'm alright. I'm here with Sabine." Turning, Vespers gestured back over to a woman standing before a stand filled with fruit and vegetables. Evan hadn't noticed her before, but looking now at her, he was acutely aware of her striking beauty and the air of sadness and solitude around her. She wore a purple dress trimmed in gold with white lace around the inside edges of the neckline and cuffs, one that seemed a touch too formal for the surroundings. Her raven hair was full and just longer than shoulder-length, pulled into a single ringlet draped over her left shoulder. Thin eyebrows poised above darkling, unfocused eyes, as though she were looking at the horizon, eyes black as midnight that seemed bored with what they beheld and yet seemed as though they should be fearsome if they fell upon one. She carried herself with a dignity and with poise but also with a sigh of isolation and she seemed dreadfully bored of her current surroundings. Her pale immaculate skin and slightly reddened cheeks were those of an elegant lady, a rich lady, Evan thought, as he continued to admire her features, a small, slender nose under those striking eyes and light red pouting, teasingly kissable lips. She was beautiful and yet, it was obvious she was alone. Even in the crowded marketplace, people seemed to naturally give her a wide birth. Evan couldn't make out any of the conversation at such a distance in a loud crowd but he could see those around her were either awkwardly trying to not take notice of her or were clumsily covering their mouths as they clearly gossiped about her.

Evan smiled. "Well, I see you've found an excellent mark. What's the plan?"

"What do you mean?" Vespers asked.

Evan looked at her like his meaning was quite plain. "When do we rob her?"

"We don't." Vespers said, looking embarrassed towards the floor for a moment. "Trust me, we don't." She paused before adding, "Besides I don't want to."

"Who is she? What's so special about her?"

"She's the owner of that château you told me to leave alone," Vespers admitted.

Evan shook his head. "So you did get caught. You're lucky to be alive. And what's with the hair?"

Vespers ran the fingers of her right hand through her now pitch black hair. "There have been a lot of changes in my life," she laughed.

"So what's this about?" Evan asked.

"I can't talk now," Vespers said. "Meet me atop the Spanish Lady tomorrow night and we'll talk."

Evan nodded as Vespers turned back to rejoin Sabine.

"The Spanish Lady" was their personal name for the Cabildo, the building built starting in 1795 to house the city council back when New Spain governed New Orleans. The Cabildo was also the site of the treaty signed between Nueva España, the Republican States and the Atlantean States of America in 1803 that formally recognized the borders of the three great nations and declared New Orleans to be a free and open port city. New Spain surrendered all rights and claims of ownership and governance to New Orleans and in exchange, the Republican and Atlantean States recognized New Orleans' independence and promised to defend her against outside aggression.

Vespers returned to the side of the strange woman and for a moment, Evan considered simply following the plan they had just arranged but, there was just something about this woman, something that made him curious and beckoned him to follow her and Vespers through the crowd for a bit, in the hopes of gathering more information about her and the strange circumstances Vespers had found herself in.

Vespers spotted him immediately and shot him a glance clearly

78

intended to warn him off but Evan paid it no mind and did his best to continue sliding through the crowd towards them. Sabine led Vespers beyond the confines of the market, enabling Evan to get a little closer but then he stopped as Sabine suddenly arrested her own pace and looked towards another woman in the crowd.

The other woman was a light-skinned Negress, or possibly a mulatto, Evan found it impossible to tell, wearing a black dress with a flower-patterned shawl around her shoulders and a brown head wrap with tan stripes. She too was beautiful and there was obviously some connection between her and Sabine as the two women locked eyes and held them for a moment. Just as quickly as it had occurred, the other woman lifted her head with a haughty flip and contemptuously proceeded on her way. By this point, Evan had gotten close enough to hear when Vespers spoke.

"Who was that woman?" she said.

Sabine walked on at a stately pace as she responded. "Oh – that's Marie Laveau. For some reason, she seems to think she's Witch Queen of New Orleans."

Evan decided better of it and thought he would make the rendezvous atop the Cabildo as planned.

* * *

Evening brought Evan pacing across the top of the old Spanish building looking out over Jackson Square waiting for Vespers to arrive. Very nearly silently, Vespers placed her hands on the edge of the roof and vaulted herself up from the edge of a window molding below.

"I wasn't sure you'd make it," Evan said.

"Why wouldn't I?"

"I don't know. I don't know what you've gotten yourself into. Where have you been Vespers? You've been gone weeks. I thought you were dead."

"I almost was. As for what I've been doing, I've been learning tantra. From Sabine."

"Sabine? That lady in the spooky old house? And what the hell is tantra?"

"It's an art form from Hindustan. The Hindustani believe that women should be above men and they serve a great eight-limbed black spider goddess of creation and destruction who weaves the flows of the aether which make up the universe. She wears the skulls of Her enemies as a garland about Her neck, yet is the most gentle and loving mother to Her children and sits atop Her husband's shaft the way a queen sits atop a throne."

"Okay – " he said in a way that communicated that he clearly didn't understand what she'd just said, "but what actually is tantra?"

"It's a means of generating and focusing aetheric flows with the circuits and currents of the body. It's a means of spiritual enlightenment achieved through artful manipulations of the flesh."

Evan blinked. "Magic. She has you thinking she's teaching you magic. She's conning you. How can *you* be conned?"

"It's not a con. It's a way of living – a means of enlightenment. It's very beautiful. Here – give me your hand."

Evan walked over to her and gave her his hand. Vespers closed her eyes and traced in circles around his palm.

"Think of yourself as a pool. A pool composed of many currents. The wind blows across the surface of the water and that water flows across the water beneath it. The sun heats those layers of the water through which it courses causing it to rise. Some of the water flows beneath the shadow of a tree and cools and sinks down. So the pool has many currents – it's not

80

ubiquitous. Some of those currents, most of them in you, flow in a male or masculine direction but some of them flow in a female or feminine direction. Every force contains within it some small measure of its opposite. So when your flows contact mine – they flow together speeding both."

Evan could feel a certain something in his hand, not just the movement of her finger across his skin but a tingling sensation, like something coming to the surface of his entire hand, something that had always been there but that he had never been aware of.

"You're doing this," he accused. "You're putting the idea in my head and my imagination is running away with me."

Vespers smiled. "I am doing it. But it's not a trick. Look – a steam engine operates through the manipulation of the Four Elements. Fire is applied to earth, in this case coal, and used to heat water, which rises into the air as steam. This steam can then be used to do work. Understand?"

"Okay."

"Okay – when two bodies join together – " she stopped tracing circles around his palm and interlocked her fingers with his, " – it creates heat. Not just a physical heat, but a spiritual heat, an aetheric heat, and just like a steam engine, that heat can be made to do work."

Evan asked, "Magic?"

"If you like," Vespers said. "One word is as good as another. It's a kind of magic. There are others. But the wonderful thing is – these currents in our bodies are like flywheels that can learn to spin faster and faster – so when we join – consciously join for that purpose – the wheels of our bodies – called chakras – gain a little more spin which allows us to do that much more aetheric work."

Vespers opened her eyes. Evan looked deeply into them. He could

81

feel a swirling current rising between the two of them, like an immaterial wind coursing through and around them both. Suddenly afraid for a moment, he pulled away from her.

"And the spooky lady taught you how to do this? That's what you've been doing these past few weeks?" Evan asked.

"Yes." Vespers nodded.

"And you couldn't get word to me? You couldn't find me or tell me? I thought you were dead, Vespers," he said.

"I'm sorry Evan. Last night was the first time I'd been out of the château since I went there that night. Sabine had said I'd done very well with my studies and I asked her if we could go out. I was lucky you ran into me when you did. She doesn't like to go out very much."

Evan looked away for a moment.

"This – " he began.

"Tantra."

Evan continued. "This tantra – this Sabine is teaching it to you. You're practicing it with her."

"Yes."

"But I thought you said it worked like a galvanic cell – the difference between two poles, male and female, generated a current."

Vespers nodded. "That's one way of looking at it, yes."

"Well then – " Evan's expression revealed the awkwardness he was feeling, "how does that work with two women? Add fire to fire, you don't get steam. Add water to water, you don't get steam."

"You're thinking too literally – the friction of two aetheric bodies interpenetrating one another generates aetheric heat which is all that is needed to create a flow to do work. And of course, focus is needed to give that flow

82

form and shape. Friction is a bad metaphor. It's like looping coils of flows between one person and another and a motive force being generated by the arcs and interstices of those flows interacting with one another. The point is to find those in some way complimentary to oneself so as to generate the greatest amount of aetherial flow."

"And that most complimentary flow – that's love?"

"No, of course not. Just because two people interact most efficiently on a physiological and spiritual basis – hmm." Vespers paused to think for a moment. "Maybe you do have a point. Look, it's complicated."

"I see that," Evan said.

"And then there's the issue of essentialism – whether or not males and females have intrinsically different souls – on which Sabine and I agree – and the issue of whether or not male/female relations are particularly sanctified by virtue of being life-affirming, on which we disagree."

"So..." Evan began.

"So?"

"So do you love her?"

"Who? Sabine? No." Vespers laughed. "She's just training me. There's nothing to get jealous about."

Evan said, "I'm not jealous."

"Are you sure? Cause you sound jealous," Vespers said.

"I am not jealous," he repeated.

"Good. Cause you're not my man and there's nothing to be jealous about, anyway. Look – I've got to get back to the château. We have prayers before dawn."

"Zoe," Evan said, using her real name, "don't go. Don't go back there. What are you getting yourself into?"

Vespers looked away from him. "I don't want to be ordinary."

"What?" Evan asked, genuinely confused.

She took a deep breath and then turned to face Evan. "I don't want to be ordinary. And Sabine has mastered skills that let her do extraordinary things. She's willing to teach me how to do extraordinary things. This is my chance to get off the streets. This is *our* chance to get off the streets."

"What do you mean?"

"I mean, I want you to study with her too."

"Me?" Evan blinked.

"Yes. We've been friends for a long time. I don't want you to leave my life now."

"I'm not the one leaving," Evan said. He started to say more and then didn't. After a moment he started again. "Will I ever see you again?"

"Don't be so melodramatic. Of course you will." Vespers affected a weak smile.

Evan wanted to do likewise but found he could not. "Take care of yourself Zoe."

"You too, Evan."

Vespers gave him a quick peck on the cheek, went over to the edge of the roof and slid down the rain gutter to be swallowed up into the night. Evan stood there pondering all he had seen, heard and experienced, unable to make sense of it all.

* * *

"Are you ready?" Sabine called out to Vespers. "We have to complete the *puja* before dawn."

"Yes," Vespers responded. "Come in and tell me if I've got this on right."

Sabine pushed open the door to Vespers room to see Vespers clad in the orange sari she'd laid out for her. The garment was made of silk, decorated with images of flowers and embroidered along its edges. Sabine herself was clad in a similar silken garment, purple in color, ornamented with little white blossoms.

"What do you think?" Vespers asked as she spun in place. The top of the garment slid partially open with Vespers' motion and for a moment, her breast was visible.

Sabine turned her head away from Vespers slightly. "You're wearing it too loosely."

Vespers looked down and seeing that her breast was exposed, pulled the garment together over her bosom. She turned away from Sabine towards the mirror on the dresser. Sabine walked into the room behind her and adjusted the fit of the sari. Sabine slid her hand down along the edge of the embroidery from Vespers shoulder, down across her breast to her stomach, holding the garment in place as she reached over and tugged the other edge of the sari further over under the belt holding it all in place. Sabine slid her hand out of the dress and tightened the belt.

"There you go," Sabine said, with a smile.

Vespers looked at herself in the mirror and beamed. She had never before worn something so elegant. Wearing a sari made her feel like a princess. She could almost forget all the years she'd spent on the street, all the times she and Evan had run from the law or some mark they had robbed, the dirt and the fear, the cold and the being hungry. Vespers wiped away the beginnings of tears before they could become a flood.

"You look beautiful," Sabine said.

Vespers turned to Sabine and throwing her arms around her waist, hugged her closely.

"Thank you," Vespers said, "for everything."

"You're perfectly welcome." Sabine said. "Let's adjourn to the temple room. We need to get started."

The two of them made their way through Sabine's château to a special room Sabine kept for prayer, within it, against the north wall on a stone pedestal, was a six-foot tall statue of Kali, Sabine's patron. The statue depicted a six-armed female figure with red eyes, holding a sword, a severed head and a bowl beneath the severed head. The figure depicted wore no articles of clothing but was adorned with a crown, various necklaces, bracelets and anklets, and most notably, a garland of skulls about Her neck. Those hands of the statue that held no articles were shown in various meditative gestures Sabine had instructed Vespers were called *mudras*.

On the floor before the pedestal, were two plush cushions. Sabine gestured to the one of the pillows and Vespers sat as instructed, lotus style.

Sabine crossed the otherwise empty room to a closet and withdrew from it a short table on small round legs. This she placed in front of the pedestal before returning to the closet. The second time she returned with a silver tray with all manner of ritual accoutrements upon it. Lastly, Sabine retrieved a red altar cloth from the closet, which she draped over the altar table before joining Vespers on the other pillow cushion on the floor. Typically, when they did *puja* together, Vespers would be the one to set everything out but this time was special.

"Close your eyes," Sabine said, and Vespers did as she was bidden. "Breathe deeply. Draw your breath in, let it out, slowly. Breathe in, breathe out. Breathe in, breathe out. Focus yourself on your breathing and your calm. Be at peace. Focus on your base chakra, your root chakra, at the base of your spine.

This is the source of your body's power. Imagine a spinning red ball glowing brighter as you tap into your strength. Above it, in your lower abdomen, is your sacral chakra, the seat of your passions and emotions. Envision it as an orange ball of light. This orange light is all of your desires within you. Your navel chakra is the seat of your will power, your personal drive to succeed and achieve. See it as a bright warm golden light. Above it, your heart chakra glows with a green, growing light. This verdant light is your center, your power to grow, to achieve harmonious relationships with others and to provide healing, both to others and yourself. Your throat, or aetheric chakra, is your center of communication, both with people and with spirits. It glows with a piercing yet soft blue light of clarity. Your creativity shines here. Your third eye chakra is indigo in color. It governs your intuition and connaissance. At the very top of your head is your crown chakra. It shines with a purple light and is your means of connection with the deep Void, the universe itself and the Goddess in all Her forms. A human body is a complex mechanism, more complicated and intricate than any watchmaker's toy and infinitely more versatile. Tuned and used correctly, it is the only tool you will ever need and with it, you can achieve things other people would call miracles if they could come to accept them at all. This is the path we walk, unity of mind and body and soul, to achieve all that humanity is meant to achieve, and more. This is the path of tantra. Open your eyes."

Vespers opened her eyes from the chakra meditation to see Sabine reaching for the silver tray. Sabine drew a long match and lit it, using it to light a small cone of incense and a lamp containing, *ghee*, clarified butter. Shaking the match to extinguish it, she then lifted up a small striker and gong and holding the gong in the air before her, struck it twice rapidly in succession. Pausing between she tapped out four pairs of soundings from the gong before

87

returning it to the silver tray.

Reaching into one of the little bowls on the tray's surface, Sabine then made three tiny piles of rice grains before the statue in offering. She then made a recitation in Sanskrit to Ganesha, elephant God of openings and remover of obstacles. Vespers bowed her head and held her hands before her, palms together, during the recitation knowing what the words were for even if she did not yet understand them.

"All things exist and no things exist," Sabine began. "All things are comprised of consciousness, the streams and rivulets of flowing aether and thus all that can be said to exist does so within the mind, the body, the soul of our beloved Mother. We are Her dream as She is ours. The womb and night are one; they are the fountains of creation. Blackness is blackness: the ocean depths, the night sky between the stars, can one said to be different from the other? We are forged in darkness, spend nine long months cradled by it. The Mother of Stars births us from the darkness in which we were created. Mystery, wonder and infinity are all as black as our Divine Mother. We are the children of the ever-flowing and fragrant Void and our Mother, Kali, is its inebriating darkness."

Sabine stood and rubbed a little of a purple pigment across the top of the statue's forehead. Likewise she then traced a small crescent on Vespers' forehead and then her own. "My sect uses a purple crescent as our *tilak*, or mark, to signify that we draw our strength from the dark of the moon."

Sabine then placed several offerings before the statue: grains of cotton and coriander seed and fingers of dried turmeric root. She then removed the stopper from a small bottle of perfume. Within the top of the bottle was a small rod which when the bottle was closed, descended into the perfume. This she shook before the statue three times before returning the stopper to the bottle. Returning the perfume bottle to the silver tray, Sabine then lay several deeply scarlet hibiscus flowers on the altar before the statue. Vespers thought to herself how perfect a symbol of the union of female and male they were – the five open petals of the flower itself and the long, shaft-like pistil and stamens rising up from its core.

After laying the hibiscus before the statue of the Goddess, Sabine waved the smoldering incense in the air before the statue and then the *glee* lamp and placed a small bowl with chunks of coconut meat in it before the statue in offering.

"Let us meditate for a time on the nature of the Void," Sabine said, "the soul of the Deep and our connection to the Goddess. Open yourself to the Void and the rapturous splendor Beyond."

Vespers closed her eyes. Meditation was still new to her and she did the best she could. She slowed her breathing and tried to empty her conscious mind, envisioning the starry night sky above the ceiling of the château. In her mind's eye, she felt herself lifted up, buoyed up, upon the currents of night-time aether, and felt that new sensation of stillness in the center of being. The calm and the quiet, both, were renewing, rejuvenating. She felt embraced by the Night, encouraged by it and its infinite blackness to shine as the little star she was, all the more brightly.

Once again, Sabine tapped out four pairs of percussive notes on the gong and Vespers returned from her meditations.

"The *puja* is now concluded. I welcome you, Vespers, I welcome you as my chela and I welcome you to my home. Please consider this as your home and temple." Sabine smiled warmly.

Vespers was beaming. She nodded gratefully. "Thank you." Vespers threw her arms about Sabine and the two of them hugged affectionately.

Sabine stood and taking Vespers by the hand, led her over to the window and pulled open the shades with her other hand. The first rays of morning light began to stream in crimson, orange and yellow across the horizon and silently the two women stood bathed in its light.

* * *

Morning found Sabine and Vespers aboard a ferry taking them across the Mississippi to the Algiers Aerodrome. Sabine was smiling for once, clad in a crimson dress with matching red leather shoes, a black over-bust corset worn over the dress, and a tiny round hat traced delicately with lace. On her forehead, she wore a small brass key-shaped bindi. Her hands she adorned with red and black fingerless lace gloves. Her flying goggles she wore about her neck and a fox fur about her shoulders.

Sabine shaded herself with a parasol in one hand and spied across the water using a pair of opera glasses with the other. Vespers was more modestly dressed in a white blouse and blue denim overalls, a neckerchief, goggles and boots. She wore a tool belt about her waist – more for appearance's sake than out of any thought that she would attempt or be allowed to attempt their use on the trip.

The Algiers Aerodrome was a flat patch of land on the West Bank of the Mississippi, a large grass-covered field with a few surrounding buildings and towers for the maintenance and staging of airships. Here moored among the other airships was Sabine's small personal airship, the *Bacchante*. *Bacchante* was a modest craft with a central boat-hulled main body and two overhead arms reaching out from a central pillar down to wheeled pontoons on her sides. The central pillar held both her single aetheric lift engine and a powered rotor. Twin propellers aft lent their might to the central rotor for forward flight. Vespers hoped she was as fast and as nimble as she looked.

90

The pilot and crew had the boilers hot and the engine going by the time Sabine and Vespers had gotten aboard. They brought only themselves and since there was no cargo to stow, they took off as soon as Sabine gave the pilot the signal. The central lift engine began to emit a low, oscillating sound while the rotor began to spin faster and faster. Smoke lazily floated out of the two short stacks on *Bacchante*'s stern above her under-deck boilers. Vespers and Sabine stood out on deck outside the tiny bridge as *Bacchante* took off. Vespers clutched a hand grip on the outside of the bridge tightly with her right hand as the craft ascended with a slight shudder. Even so, the gleaming smile on her face spoke of at least as much excitement as fear. Sabine held neither one of the hand grips nor the railing around the edge of the small airship as they lifted free of the ground and floated slowly towards the heavens.

Vespers looked out across the field as they ascended, taking in the view of the other airships, both those grounded and those floating over the field tethered to one of the towers on the perimeter. She lifted her gaze as they floated further and further from the ground to take in the scope of the cerulean sky dotted with white patches of cottony clouds. She had always dreamt of flying and here she actually was – sharing the sky with the birds and the Sun, soaring amongst the clouds. Vespers let go of the hand-grip and took a few cautious steps across the airship's deck. Their ascent was graceful and slow and she had no problem keeping her footing. She moved towards the bow of the ship and Sabine with her.

Placing her hands on the railing, Vespers leaned forward and spied down from the bow to the river below. Steamships, ferries and fishing boats plied their way across and down the Mississippi's ancient waters indifferent to the mighty craft floating high above. Vespers looked out across the city to the French Quarter and Jackson Square. Her eyes lingered on the roof of the

Cabildo, wondering if Evan could see her now. She sighed, lending a pause to her elation, but only a momentary one.

"Here," Sabine said.

When Vespers turned, Sabine was holding a single peacock's feather in her hand. She took it. The feather was a scintillating collage of blues, yellows and greens with a gorgeous multi-colored eye visible on its delicate features.

"What's it for?" she asked.

Sabine shrugged, smiling in that way that Vespers had learned to interpret as "Figure it out."

Taking the feather gingerly between index finger and thumb, Vespers watched it bend back and forth in the breeze. The motion of the ship changed as the ship ceased its purely vertical ascent and the pitch of the rotor tilted forward, sending *Bacchante* straight ahead into the open blue.

Vespers' attention returned to the feather, watching the air flutter it back and forth in her hand. She pulled it close to her mouth and blew at it, spying the change in the feather's motion. She swung her hand through the air in figure eights with the feather. Bringing it close to her eyes, she looked over its tiny multi-colored variations as the wind continued to blow it back and forth in her hand. Her heart pounded in her chest and in a moment of caprice, she simply let the feather go. Vespers' gaze followed the graceful form of the feather as it spun and swirled in the breeze. She felt the wind caress her skin and wondered what it must be like for the feather.

Closing her eyes, she let go of the railing and stood firm on the deck of the airship, reaching outwards with her mind. She found the feather there, the scene she had closed her eyes to replicated in her mind. She saw as the feather might have, was the feather. The currents of the wind buffeted her about from one to another. She danced in circles upon the soul of the air and was elated by it. No happiness she had ever known compared to this. She threw open her arms and laughed, suddenly aware of this tiny torrent of air and that, this wayward breeze and that sudden gust of air. She was part of the living ocean of the sky, part of its permanent and yet momentary cerulean majesty. It was as though she had become the very breath of God.

Vespers stumbled forward and grabbed the railing with both hands. She grew dizzy and started to fall backwards but Sabine was waiting there and caught her about the waist. Vespers steadied herself, clutching at Sabine's hands, aware of her racing heart and her now rapid breathing. Still holding onto Sabine's hands, she turned and looked up into Sabine's face and as their eyes met, Vespers gasped, slightly and quietly, and felt her face flush. There was a moment of clarity, of total understanding between them when words were not required and the sounds of the airship faded away, a moment of perfect silence between the two women.

"It's – " Vespers started.

"A larger world than you realized?" Sabine finished.

Vespers nodded.

"I felt that way too," Sabine smiled. "Well done. We should head back." Sabine circled a finger in the air to let the pilot know they were ready to return. Slowly, the graceful little craft began to bank back towards Algiers.

* * *

That night, Vespers lay awake in bed. She just roused herself from dozing off. In bed with her was a dictionary of Sanskrit and the *Yoga Spandakarika*. Sabine was teaching her Sanskrit and had insisted that while the *Yoga Spandakarika* was an important part of her studies, that she should only read it in the original Sanskrit, which Vespers was finding to be slow going at

93

best. "Vivardhayati," she said aloud as she checked its meaning in the hand-written dictionary Sabine had given her. "To cause to grow, increase or lengthen." Her finger traced down further. "To cut, sever or reduce." She shut the dictionary with a loud clap.

"How can a word mean both something and its opposite?" Vespers asked aloud. Tossing the bed-sheet to one side, she swung her legs over the side of the bed and put her feet in her slippers resolved to see if Sabine was awake and could help her with the matter.

Carrying the unwieldy dictionary with her as she went, Vespers went up the stairs from the second story to the third, where Sabine's rooms were. The bottom floor of the château was dedicated to the parlor, the kitchen, the butler's pantry, the game room, the grand foyer, disused servants' quarters, the laundry room, the music room and the ballroom. The second floor held guest bedrooms, a disused children's play room, the sauna and spa and now Vespers' room. The third floor held Sabine's personal library, her temple room, bedroom, her painting room and rooms she used for personal storage.

Tucking the book under her left arm, Vespers made her way to Sabine's personal quarters. The door to the room was cracked open a tad and as Vespers approached and lifted her hand to knock on the door, she suddenly stopped. Vespers exhaled and knocked twice on the door.

"Come in," Sabine said.

Vespers entered the room and pulled a chair over besides the bed and sat down. She plopped the large, worn hand-written Sanskrit dictionary on to the edge of the bed.

"Working on your studies, I see," Sabine said with a smile. "That's good."

The wind picked up again outside and the draft blew across where

94

Vespers was sitting and she shivered. Sabine rolled back the edge of the blanket facing Vespers and said, "Get in."

Vespers pulled the large tome off the edge of the bed and placed it on the chair, and kicking off her slippers, slid in under the blanket next to Sabine.

Vespers nodded. "I'm having trouble with this word – vivardhayati."

Sabine said, "It means to draw out." She pantomimed pulling a thread out from a spool.

Vespers nodded again. "I saw that – it means to lengthen but it also means to cut off or sever?"

"It can mean causing a break in something by pulling on it," she pantomimed again, "like tearing a piece of taffy by pulling it out. I think."

"You think?" Vespers smiled.

The two women laughed.

"So how are your studies going otherwise?" Sabine asked.

"Well enough, I think," Vespers said. "Although..." Vespers abruptly stopped, suddenly self-conscious about what she was feeling.

"Although what?" Sabine asked. And when Vespers didn't say anything, she put her book back on the night stand and said, "You can say whatever you want here. I won't mind. I want you to be honest with me. The only rule is that you make your meaning plain."

"I just feel like I should be thanking you," Vespers said. "I mean, I know I only took you up on apprenticeship because, well, because you gave me no choice."

"Sorry," Sabine said sheepishly. "But you were – "

Vespers put her hands up. "I know." She looked away for a moment. "But I feel like you did me the greatest favor in the world. If I had only known what was out there, I would have leapt at the opportunity." Vespers turned and hugged Sabine tight.

A few moments passed wordlessly, with nothing more than the satisfying holding of each other in their arms and the rising and falling of breathing before Sabine spoke.

"Thank you," Sabine said.

"For what?" Vespers asked.

"For this. For being my chela, for sharing yourself, your time, with me. I needed this. I'd been alone for so long, I'd forgotten what it was to not be lonely." Sabine kissed Vespers on the forehead.

"There's a whole world out there, Sabine, you don't have to stay cooped up in this house all the time."

Sabine shook her head. "Sweet Vespers, It's not my world out there. And I'm afraid I've gotten used to having my way. No. What happens beyond these walls is no concern of mine. Not as long as my little world stays safe."

Vespers opened her mouth to object and decided that there would be another time for that discussion.

* * *

Evan found a note waiting for him when he returned to his "lair," the basement of a boarding house outside Storyville. Fortune had smiled upon him and his take from tourists and travelers through the city had been good and so the converted basement apartment was somewhat less than his means could afford but Evan considered it unwise to draw attention to himself by securing better lodging. He read over the note which instructed him to meet Vespers again atop the Spanish Lady.

Evan reached the rooftop first, as he usually did when meeting Vespers and awaited her arrival. Fortunately, he didn't have to wait long and hearing Vespers scale the side of the building, he reached down and offered her a hand up. Vespers alighted upon the roof and Evan stepped back to give her more room.

"How have you been, Evan?" Vespers asked.

"I'm doing well. I've almost got enough money to open that tinker's shop I always wanted to." Evan's gaze lowered to the roof. That he always envisioned it being their tinker's shop, he left unspoken.

"And, uh, the guys?"

"Hercule and Easy Jack are doing alright. Steamboat Pete was shot by a riverboat gambler in an argument over poker. He didn't make it."

"I guess we always knew it was going to happen. He just wouldn't stop. Gambling, cheating – making terrible bets. And Sarah?"

"Even with all the gambling, he'd left enough money to look after her. She won't get it all until she turns twenty-one but some of it was released to her immediately. She's already in a boarding school up north."

"That's good," Vespers said.

Evan nodded in agreement.

The two of them stood in silence for a while. The shadow of a passing airship fell across them and then slid away.

"So – " Vespers paused for a while before continuing. "Have you been with anyone yet?"

"What?"

"Have you – "

"I heard you," Evan said, cutting her off. "Did you really ask me to meet you here to find out if I'd slept with anyone yet?"

"Um, yes," Vespers laughed. "So?"

"You know you're strange, right? Anyway – the answer to your question – not that's any of your business – is no. I mean, a couple of the Storyville girls offered but I don't want my first time to be with one of them." It was Evan's turn for an awkward pause. "Have you?"

"No," Vespers said.

There was silence and the darkening of Evan's complexion.

"Huh," she said, "I didn't know blacks could blush."

Evan muttered incoherently.

"You don't have to be embarrassed." Vespers turned around and slapped herself on the ass twice. "I'd be glad to make a man of you."

Evan scowled. "I am a man."

Vespers softened. "Of course you are sweetie. I'm sorry. That was poorly phrased. I only meant that I would be happy to relieve you of the burden of your virginity."

"Um," Evan began, "and I can't believe I'm even asking this – but why?"

Vespers turned away from him and looked out over Jackson Square. "I like you. I mean, I've always liked you. You and I – we were close. I trust you – and I've missed you these past few weeks. I've missed being close to you. Why should there be anything more than that? Sabine's taught me that when two people make love – not just have sex – but consciously and truly make love – there is a joining, a sharing – their minds and bodies and souls are awakened to something more sublime and afterwards, the two are made greater thereby." She turned back around to face him. "That's something I'd like to experience – with you."

There was a long pause in which neither of them said anything.

"I care about you too, Zoe. I always have."

Vespers smiled. "Then, be with me. Please."

"Okay."

Evan pulled her close and kissed her sweetly on the lips. "I can't believe you said 'please.' Like there was a chance I was going to say no."

"Oh, I don't know," Vespers said. "You can be stubborn, after all."

"I suppose that's true."

The two of them kissed again and then began to make their way off the roof of the Cabildo towards Sabine's château. Reaching the house, they went up the stairs to the second floor and down the corridor to Vespers' room. She placed a hand upon the door.

"Now, it's a work in progress," she said.

"Understood," Evan replied.

Vespers pushed the door open to reveal an almost jet black room, black wooden floors with black furniture, a sofa, dresser and chairs, a black edged mirror on the wall, the walls themselves covered in black on grey filigree wallpaper. Even the bed sheets were black. The bed and the sofa had red pillows laying atop them and the windows were flanked with black drapes. A single chandelier descended from the ceiling covered in half-melted candles and there was an oil lamp on the night stand along with a number of large, heavy looking books.

"She let you redecorate," Evan said.

"How could you tell?" Vespers asked with a smile. She closed the door behind Evan as he entered the room and then kicked off her shoes and sat down on the edge of the bed. Vespers patted the bed next to her, coaxing Evan to sit beside her and he did, albeit looking uncomfortable as he did so. Evan kicked off his own shoes.

"What's wrong?" Vespers asked.

"Nothing. I'm just a little nervous."

"You don't have to be nervous," Vespers said.

"You say that, but I've never done this before."

"I haven't either, you know." Vespers paused. "Do you trust me?"

"Of course I do," Evan said.

Vespers smiled. "Then place yourself entirely in my hands."

Evan nodded his assent.

Vespers pulled herself onto Evan's lap and straddled him, taking the buttons of his shirt into her fingers and nimbly undoing them one by one. As she did so, she would occasionally glance upwards into Evan's eyes, watching his ardor grow from anticipation. Pulling his shirt off of him, she slid her warm palms across his naked chest and pushed him gently back into the bed. Evan closed his eyes, giving himself over to her completely. Vespers leaned down and drew her tongue across his abdomen in long, lingering strokes, licking here and there, feeling Evan tremble at her touch. She licked upwards along his chest and across his nipples. She climbed forward to kiss him passionately on the mouth and then withdrew to kiss him down the nape of his neck. Evan took her hair into his fist and held her tightly around the waist with the other arm pulling her into him with the pleasure of it. Vespers ground the softness of her derrière against the growing hardness trapped in Evan's trousers.

Vespers took one of his nipples between her thumb and forefinger and pinched down hard and Evan arched his back towards her in response, keeping his eyes closed. Vespers grinned wickedly at his pleasure and open vulnerability. She traced her fingertips gently across the skin of his chest and giggling, leaned down to bite gently on the other nipple, relishing in Evan's shuddering. She kissed him on the mouth again as her fingers worked to undo his belt and the buttons of his trousers.

Evan opened his eyes and reached to undo Vespers' garments and she drew his fingers down his face indicating she wanted him to keep his eyes closed and Evan did as she bid him. Smirking with a sudden inspiration, Vespers drew a handkerchief from out of her pocket and tied it as a blindfold over Evan's eyes. She then pulled Evan's trousers and underpants off of him, he lifting his buttocks to let the garments slip free from his form.

Vespers pulled her leg across Evan's lap and hopped off the bed. Rummaging through a drawer, she withdrew two long silk scarves and returned to the bed. She slammed his left wrist to the headboard and tied him to it with one scarf before attending to the other wrist. Then she stood slowly and left him to wait as she undressed herself on the far side of the room, letting her garments fall to the floor, one by one. Vespers sashayed her way back to the bed, crept upon it and crawled over Evan's helpless form. Smiling as she surveyed his face, Vespers curled her fingers about his erect member and began to stroke it gently up and down. Evan's mouth fell open and his head back, his hips moving unbidden up and down with the motion of her hand upon his manhood.

Vespers leaned over Evan's lingam and pushed a thin stream of saliva out of her mouth with her tongue, drizzling it across the tip of his erect shaft. She rubbed her hand all over the tip of Evan's manhood to lubricate her hand and continued her massaging of him afterwards. Feeling excited herself, she took her other hand and placed two fingers within and satisfied with the wetness she found there, took that hand and rubbed Evan gently behind his testicles. Evan quivered and writhed, moaning loudly as she did so. Vespers stroked him once, twice more and then, holding him by the base of his shaft, took him into her mouth.

Pulling her head forward along his length, her tongue cradling his manhood as she did so, Vespers bobbed her head up and down, pulling and sucking on him as she moved. Evan involuntarily pulled against his bonds, but they and his blindfold held despite the motion of his body. He fell back gently against the head board, rolling his head side to side as Vespers worked his shaft. Vespers leaned back and then slowly pushed forward all the way as far as she could until her lips reached the base of him and then she placed her teeth against the skin of his member and raked gently back as she withdrew her head.

Evan inhaled sharply. "Ahh..."

Vespers leaned back and continued to work his hard erection with her hand.

Whispering, Vespers said, "Tell me what you want."

"I want you – I want to caress and hold you – I want to ravish you outdoors in the heat of a summer's night – I want to ravish you in snow. I want to kiss you, to stroke your skin – I want to devour your flesh. I want to have you and make you mine – I want to possess you utterly."

Vespers froze for a moment astonished at Evan's words before she pulled the blindfold from his eyes and undid the knots at his wrists. Evan seized her by the wrists in a single heartbeat and pulled her to him to kiss her wildly upon the mouth. He thrust his tongue into the soft wetness of Vespers' mouth, meeting hers and sliding his tongue under and over hers. Evan pushed Vespers down to the bed, moving atop her. He entered her with one fierce stroke, Vespers' gasp rising loudly to his ears as he did so and he thrust into her, again and again and again, like a man possessed.

Evan rode Vespers with the passion and vigor of a young man, her lithe arms wrapped around his neck, her legs gripping him around his hips, pulling him deeper into her with his every masculine stroke. Her lustful, sweet cries of gratification further enthralled and inspired Evan as he, sweating, plumbed the depths of her yoni. Holding back as long as he could, Evan's seed burst forth from him in ecstasy as he let forth a mighty roar.

Evan opened his eyes to utter blackness. There was nothing. Not even himself. Void.

A girl, laughing, picking flowers in a meadow.

A young woman.

The young woman bent and curved and he with her. The two moving like snakes and then intertwining into a lemniscate.

The young woman and he as a spider – his four limbs and her four limbs together, crawling across the too-green grass of an unknown landscape.

Blackness once more.

Evan saw himself caught on a tree, his wrists bound by its branches, his ankles likewise held.

Evan was the tree.

The young woman was caught upon him, her wrists and ankles bound by his branches.

He grew through her – his branches grew through her. She screamed, not in pain but in ecstatic joy. He grew through her wrists and her ankles. He grew through the base of her spine. He grew up the length of her spine and out of her belly button. He grew out of her yoni and her thighs and her knees and her feet. He grew through her ribs and her lungs and her heart and her shoulders and her elbows and hands. He grew up through her throat and a branch of him grew out of her mouth – and a great, verdant radiance shined forth from out of her mouth and her eyes and all there was – everywhere – was green light – that immense verdant shining that filled Her and shone through Her eyes and from Her mouth – and it shone from His bark and His branches and His roots and His leaves – and He was Shiva, She was Kali and together, together, they were the World.

There was laughter and He thought-felt...*You aware of Me...Me of You...keeping an eye on You...farewell*...and as the light began to recede – Evan felt Her smile lingering in his heart.

Evan's eyes fluttered open to find Vespers looking up at him with a worried expression on her face.

"Did you see?" Evan asked.

Vespers just nodded.

"Are you okay?" she asked.

"Better than," he said. "Better than."

He rolled off of her and sat up and when she turned on her side to face him, Evan impetuously scooped her up on top of him. Vespers giggled. Evan smiled and pulled her close, wrapping his arms about her as she did him and leaned his face into her breasts and the two cuddled, enjoying the sweet infinity of the warmth of each other's naked skin and the sound of each other's heartbeats and breathing.

END

Crescent City

by Jackson Kuhl

The lecture hall erupted in derision and disbelief. Lecoq allowed the roar to break over him like a wave, gripping his lapels, his head shaking side-to-side in rebuttal. Behind him, projected on the screen by the laterna magica, glowed an artist's rendition of his vision: an escalating staircase of platforms, each supporting buildings, shops, homes, trees, mooring masts — even the Saint Louis Cathedral — suspended above the earth by a framework of steel. A city in the sky.

The Academy of Sciences hissed and complained but Lecoq's booming voice answered the loudest criticisms in turn.

"It is impossible! How will you raise the existing structures?"

"By the means of hydraulic lift," said Lecoq.

"Where will you procure that much steel?"

"I have already contacted a number of steelworks in America," said Lecoq. "They are able to supply our needs and stand ready to fulfill our order."

"And what will your steel stand upon? There isn't so much as a pebble of bedrock for two-hundred miles!"

This provoked a great deal of assents and hoorays.

"Ah," said Lecoq. He nodded to the projectionist. The fellow, half-asleep, pinched his cigarette between his lips and inserted the next slide.

"Witness the new Crescent City!" Lecoq waved at the new image on the screen. "Just as the great dirigibles float overhead, so too shall we use the properties of lighter-than-air gases to thrust New Orleans heavenward. Enormous cylinders of hydrogen, airtight, will be submerged under the mud. These will be the basis upon which we build. The weight of our city, the buoyancy of the gas — perfect equilibrium. As sure a foundation as any bedrock, sir. I have everything calculated down to the last kilogram."

"Pontoons? You mean to raise our city on *pontoons?*"

"Not precisely. Pontoons float on water. These cylinders are to be suspended in the mud to prevent drift. I prefer to call them *aero-hydrogeolic tethers*. Or 'Lecoqs' for short."

"They're pontoons!"

"Well," said Lecoq, "If you insist. The principle is the same."

"The Council will never agree to it!"

But, in fact, the Superior Council did. As absurd and exorbitant as the cost was, upon tallying the damages wrought by the hurricanes of 1852, 1856, 1860, and 1879, not to mention the eighteenth-century storms of 1722, 1779, and 1780, for which exact figures were unknown but the aftermath was — in every case, the city was flattened like a pancake — the cost of raising New Orleans safely above storm surges and broken levees was far less than the amount projected to rebuild when the next hurricane hit. Lecoq's design had the added bonus of segregating the city wards to distinct platforms, which appealed to a Council mindful of the devastating fires of 1788 and 1794; plus their ascension far removed from mosquito-haunted swamps might well prevent repetitions of the yellow-fever epidemics of 1853, 1858, and 1878. Further ameliorating the expense were the charitable donors Lecoq had arranged, who came before the Council like communicants at Sunday Mass, their private funds for public works echoing the previous century's raising of the Cabildo and the Presbytère. Granted, the altruism of these elites lay on the table in exchange for choice parcels on the yet-to-be-built topmost levels of the new city. But who among the Council could sneeze at free money — whilst saving New Orleans once and for all from wrack and ruin?

So with naysayers stifled and cogs set in motion, it was a cheerful Lecoq who greeted Andre Julyan as he was ushered into his employer's office.

"Andre!" said Lecoq. "You wanted to see me, boy?"

A cloud of irritation passed over Julyan's eyes. He was married, with two young sons better befitting the diminutive. In fact, Julyan had been with the firm Paschal & Lecoq long before the senior partner, whose love of butter and beignets was surpassed only by a passion for chicory flesh, exhausted his heart during a particularly frisky romp with his Afro-Creole mistress, thereby passing the company to Lecoq's sole custodianship. Julyan was the only draftsman who remained from that time: diligent, exacting, arriving early and leaving after the rest had slipped away.

"Indeed, sir," said Julyan. "It was in regard to your plans to elevate the city. As I'm sure you're aware, there is a problem with them. A very large problem."

"Yes?" Lecoq looked up from his fussing with papers. "If you mean the risk of capsizing in high winds — like those, say, of a hurricane — then do not concern yourself. I have overcompensated by increasing the volume of the pontoons. Their buoyancy is more than enough to keep the city from tipping." He held up an illustration, showing the platforms from above in their sickle-shaped arrangement, haloed by the pontoons, invisible beneath the muck.

"No, it wasn't that," said Julyan. "You see, sir, I noticed — well, I couldn't *help* but notice your plans bear striking similarity to a set of diagrams I

107

had upon my desk in the atelier some months ago."

The room turned icy.

Lecoq stood upright, spoke sternly. "If you are suggesting I misappropriated these plans from you, then I tell you it is contrary to reason. You are an employee of my company. Therefore anything you write or draw in my employ is my property."

"But I did not draw them while in your employ, Monsieur Lecoq. That was a project I worked on after-hours, for my own amusement. Not on the firm's time."

"Regardless, you used my pencils. You used my drafting tools. Therefore — mine."

Julyan shrugged. "That is not what concerns me presently. I *abandoned* those plans because there is a catastrophic flaw in their design. To proceed would be to endanger the city and countless lives. You must know it."

"What flaw? I see none."

"No?" And Andre Julyan explained the error.

"Preposterous," said Lecoq. "I have never heard of such a phenomenon."

"I surmised your reaction would be so." Julyan withdrew an envelope from inside his coat and tossed it on the desktop. "Is your arrogance too great to consider fallibility? Certainly it is too great to accept responsibility once the project fails. You will attempt to direct blame onto someone else — perhaps the man whose work you used without consultation. I do not wish to be present when that time comes."

Lecoq's hands curled into fists; the hair stood on the back of Lecoq's neck. "Your insolence is too great to remain in my office a moment longer. Remove yourself, boy. I am terminating your employment immediately."

108

"How can you?" Julyan nodded toward the envelope. "I've already quit."

The preparations took years. First came the evictions and property seizures, the litigation and judgments and filing of motions. The human obstacles swept from the board, the trenches came next: enormous pits, their sides braced with timber, wherein the pontoons would be assembled in situ. Heavy-gauge steel, in quantities never before produced, was smelted and imported from the mountains of Pennsylvania. Workers hot-riveted hoops and braces together into skeletons for the pontoons, each as long as two city blocks, then covered them in skins of thick canvas doped with aluminum oxide, impermeable and rot-proof. Mechanical moles, their turbine-driven noses grinding and ripping like some kind of Torquemadian confession extractor, ripped open the avenues, flashed their tails at the sun, plunged into the earth. Hordes armed with shovels and picks followed. Meanwhile other teams, winding their way through a Vieux Carre torn asunder, slipped down into the mud to construct the latticework of the first platform beneath the wheels of the endless parade of carts trucking away tons of excavated muck.

For weeks and months, New Orleans pounded and throbbed, and the citizens' teeth rattled in their jaws from the incessant steam-hammers and occasional booms of dynamite. A meal could not be eaten from an unchipped plate or bowl as every piece of crockery in city limits was thrown from its cupboard daily. Visitors fled the hotels, nerves ruined. Pharmacists and voodoo priestesses cleared their shelves of headache powders and sedatives. Sleep became impossible; no sooner had one's eyelids drooped then a seismic shock lifted the bedposts off the floor. People dozed when they could. Grown men nodded at lunch tables, chins on chests; women, turning for a moment from the washtub or the stove's heat, would sit, then sprawl as exhaustion

109

overtook them. New Orleans became a city of narcoleptics, the people staggering among the rubble at midnight or passed out on benches in Jackson Square at noon.

Lecoq's legal troubles dragged just as long: Not three weeks after their encounter, Julyan filed a lawsuit against Paschal & Lecoq. But not for the reason Lecoq assumed.

"Then you do not deny the plans for Crescent City are the sole property of Paschal & Lecoq?" asked Lecoq's attorney during a particular tiresome deposition.

"No," said Julyan. "Monsieur Lecoq is welcome to them. Rather I am suing his company for gross negligence. I seek damages for losses to the reputation of the engineering trade."

The attorney scoffed in a theatrical manner. "What losses? What damage?"
"Those that will occur after the elevation fails."

This produced much laughter from everyone — except Julyan and his solicitor, of course. And yet the magistrate refused to toss the case outright, for while a loss that had yet to occur obviously could not be estimated, the hypothetical question tickled the imagination of a man bored by wading through petty accounting discrepancies and tedious bankruptcy proceedings.

"This theory as to why you believe the project is unsound, Monsieur Julyan," asked Lecoq's attorney another time, "It is yours and yours alone?"

"I have discussed it with associates," said Julyan. "Insofar as its origins, however, it is based on my own observations of soil and environment."

"So the theory is not widely shared by others?"

"Not to my knowledge."

"It is not even a *minority* opinion in scientific circles?"

"I don't believe so."

The attorney smiled. "Then how can you propose to know with certainty that Monsieur Lecoq's plan will fail when you, yourself, admit your ideas are too peripheral to exist even on the *fringes* of scientific knowledge?"

"Aren't my ideas just as valid as those of Monsieur Lecoq?" asked Julyan. "Am I not an engineer myself and the owner of a successful structural engineering company?"

This last, much to Lecoq's frustration, was true. For while Julyan was, to him and his close friends, pariah; and as much as they strove to cultivate and enforce this attitude with their own clients and business dealings, there was just too much work for Paschal & Lecoq alone. The day dawned when, with a loud thrumming of engines and erupting of smoke and groaning of metal, four square blocks between Dauphine and Royal Streets were raised centimeter by agonizing centimeter to the height of a steamship's stack. There they rested while workmen fastened fresh girders and struts to the bottom of the pylon. Once done, the machines again raised the platform to a new elevation, and the workmen again fastened new supports. When the desired height was reached, the workmen welded the final connection between truss and pontoon, resulting in a fragment of the French Quarter perched atop a tower of tetrahedrons. And while the successful conclusion showered Lecoq with back-slapping and happy hand-shaking and cigar smoke — "This day shall forever be commemorated as 'Lecoq's Day!'" he told friends — his enemy shared too in the victory, for several of the buildings along that airborne segment of Bourbon Street had had, beforehand, their foundations secured and walls reinforced by the firm of Andre Julyan, Engineer.

After the raising of the initial platform, Lecoq never slept more than four hours a night. Not because of the cacophony of construction — although there was that. But from the moment in the morning when his feet touched the floorboards, the day burst with meetings and measurements, with running across town to inspect this aspect or that excavation, with checking new drawings or conferring with foremen and vendors. Lecoq grew to enjoy the breathlessness, the urgency of his demanded presence and attention. Whereas before his celebrity was constricted to the city's upper echelon, now the commonest drudges recognized him in the streets, and bank presidents and fishwives alike gossiped about Lecoq's future ambitions.

"I think when Crescent City is done, I should like to head the Superior Council," said Lecoq at a dinner party one night, after two glasses of Bordeaux. "New Orleans has ever required a strong hand. Its placement between the river and Bayou Saint-Jean should never have been — only by a quirk of history is it situated here rather than at Bayou Manchac. And you see how the people are! Without *initiative*, without *vision*, the city would disappear into the bog as they rolled like pigs in their own vice and crapulence. It needs a Lecoq!"

Those gathered around murmured their agreement.

Yet a single thing troubled him. One of the pontoons was buried in a particularly swampy patch of bayou. On a previous visit to the site, Lecoq noted the mire reached the expected level along the pylon's base; but upon a subsequent review, he saw the water level lay a meter above its previous mark. This was well within his planned tolerance — but it was also unexpected. He returned to the site frequently, making careful calibrations. The pontoon was sound, filled with hydrogen and not leaking. The steel was not deformed. So why did it rest lower in the water than before? Then Lecoq noticed something else: the knees of a nearby bald cypress, which before had jutted above the waterline, were now almost invisible beneath the murk. He could only conjecture the entire bayou appeared to be — no, thought Lecoq. That was ridiculous.

At last the crowning platform rose into position. Crescent City was complete. Newspapers as far away as China splashed photos of the skyline across their front pages. Commerce and guests returned: Cranes laded sacks and crates onto the decks of vessels resting upon the Mississippi beneath, bound for Texas and the coasts of America; the German zeppelin *Düsseldorf* was met at the city's main mooring mast with a brass band and a salvo of confetti. The citizens, who never needed an excuse to pause labor and shed care, celebrated — celebrated the end of engineering schemes, the stoppage of jackhammers and blasting, the death of noise and concussion. Sequined mummers assembled on the lowermost platform and paraded through the streets until they arrived at the other side. They danced up the bridge to the next, and so on, up and around the half-moon shape of Julyan's design, tossing candy to bystanders, swilling from jugs passed to them from the balconies. The end of mud! For there was very little earth amongst the clouds, only enough for a roadside tree or flower garden. The end of sleeplessness! For the rarefied silence made nighttime deep and satisfying. The end of anchorage to the ground, subject to nature's whim; the end of floods and wind and levee breaks. The end of worry.

Julyan kept busy, as several of the platforms were blank squares to be filled after construction. He designed a dozen homes for well-to-doers, plus the new office for the Coffee Import Association and the meeting house of the city's small population of Quakers.

Except Julyan's architectural consultation often came with odd addendums. Strange braces. Unnecessary scaffolds hidden from view.

113

Buttresses which reinforced walls from nonexistent torque. His eccentricity compounded extra cost so these fixtures were usually ignored by the builders. But not always. The same acceptance could not be said of Julyan's lawsuit, for the magistrate, adjudging Lecoq's monument an unqualified success, tired of legal intellectualism and dismissed the case altogether.

Nothing bad ever happens at a convenient time or when people are best able to face catastrophe — never at twelve noon when a person is fit and healthy with lunch in his stomach. So of course it was at one o'clock on an October morning when Crescent City pitched sharply toward the south. There it hung for precarious moments before, steel screaming, the pylons sheared away from their pontoons and the whole semi-circle dropped into foam and mud like a launched ship sliding from its ways.

Thousands were crushed or drowned. The dazed survivors emerged from rubble and wood to climb to some high point and stare dumbfounded at an alien world. A tumulus of stones that had been the cathedral. A corner of a platform near vertical in the mud like a knife thrown into a tabletop. Mooring masts sprouting sideways, weed-covered logs above the waterline. A long berm of bricks that had been shops along Decatur. Islands and mud banks, choked between by floating wood and straw. And here and there, a semi- or nearly complete building sunk to its second story, iron-wrought balcony intact. These last had in common the name Andre Julyan, Engineer.

Some months later, Julyan sat down at the table adjacent to Lecoq. It was an outdoor café, crude and makeshift, where Lecoq had sought a minute's refuge from the solicitors and warrants and harassment; if before he barely dozed because of demand, now he staggered bloodshot-eyed from jerry-rigged courthouse to subpoena to shipwrecked office, attempting always to extricate himself and set things aright. He slumped in his chair, holding his

114

collar tight, hoping no one would recognize him.

The café, set upon a low pile of timbers and shingles, overlooked a wide canal between ridges. Tumbledown, detritus-made shacks — Julyan recognized the sign of the Coffee Import Association in one roof — ran along their lengths. Smoke from small cook fires drifted slowly toward the sky, cautious and reluctant.

"Five-hundred fifty million tonnes," said Lecoq to Julyan. "Isn't that what you said? Five-hundred fifty million tonnes of sediment."

"Every year," said Julyan. "Dumped by the Mississippi outside the mouth of the river."

"Silt and sand. Fine grains, like table salt. Yet the weight of it enough to warp and distort the landscape."

Julyan said, "This whole part of the continent is descending like a scale of a measuring balance. A grain at a time, slowly sinking. We can only cling to it like water bugs, standing on the surface tension."

Lecoq shook his head, amazed. The pontoons had sunk not because of a deficiency in his calculations — they had sunk because the mud *around* them had sunk, buried under tons of fresh mud carried from upstream by the river, taking the pontoons with it.

"I suppose decades from now this will be known as a 'Lecoq,'" he said. "'The Lecoq Affair' or 'Lecoq's Folly.'"

Out on the canal, a man in a pirogue ferried passengers between the span. Another fellow poled a raft along the banks, selling beignets and hot coffee from a cooking pot.

"*Lecoq* will become synonymous with *murderer* and *madman*," said Julyan. "But with any luck your name will be overshadowed by something else. Something new. Something not yet seen on this side of the world."

Beyond the edge of the deck, a woolly man pulled the oars of a rowboat. Stacked in the stern was a pyramid of wire hutches full of chickens.

The man saw Lecoq and Julyan watching him, scrutinizing his cargo.

"This is how it starts!" he called, smiling. "I sell half the eggs for cakes and breads, the other half I grow into more chickens. Soon I'll be the chicken king of New Orleans. Vision, gentlemen! You gotta have initiative and vision!"

The man rowed on, cackling to himself.

END

You Gotta Give Good...

By C.M. Beckett

Shadows rippled across the page of Charlotte Lacroix's book as the flame from the gaslamp fluttered above her head. Outside, she could hear a clamor of voices. Charlotte closed her book and got up to investigate. As she did, a spring released and clockwork gears churned to life in the corner of the room.

"It's okay T.O.M.A.S. There's no need for you to get up," said Charlotte, and she stepped outside.

The heavy air pressed against her dark flesh, popping beads of sweat down the backs of her arms. The surrounding homes were quiet, Charlotte's neighbors more forgiving of the hot New Orleans nights than she.

A few minutes later Charlotte came to the edge of town where a small mob had formed – as many men holding pints of beer as pitchforks and torches. Charlotte – lean and wiry with long braids and sharp, piercing eyes – approached the men, who were focused toward the middle of their circle.

Edmand Renaud, a large, pale man with bushy white hair and piercing eyes, turned to address Ms. Lacroix. "We don't need your kind here," he said, as he moved to block her path.

"I be goin' through you if I cain't go around," said Charlotte.

The large man hesitated, but quickly relented. Charlotte pushed to the edge of the mob and all eyes turned to her – the vigor draining from their faces.

Jacques Renaud – Chief Constable, younger brother to Edmand, taller and leaner than his elder sibling – stood in the middle of the group, his truncheon swinging ominously over a black man wearing a frayed Confederate uniform.

Charlotte stepped into the middle of the circle and glared at the constable. "I see," she said. "This man be some great and powerful threat, all beat and bloodied as he is."

"You have no right being here," said Jacques.

"I gots every right," said Charlotte. "We a free city and ain't nobody turned away if they need help."

Charlotte pushed past the younger Renaud and knelt by the soldier. Close up, she could see welts covering his bare arms and dried blood caked on his face. The man was haggard, struggling for breath. She ran her fingers over his shoulders.

"He gots a hex on him," said Charlotte. She turned to the crowd, found a friendly face. "Isaac. Bring some o' dem peaches," she said to an older man, nodding to the tree behind him. "Hurry."

Jacques Renaud stepped closer, glaring down at Charlotte. "Do not act in a manner you may regret later."

"I gots no worries, Constable," said Charlotte. "What your conscience tellin' you?"

Jacques Renaud raised his truncheon and held it for a long moment, but chose not to act on his rage.

Isaac knelt down beside Charlotte and handed her the fruit. "Thank Papa you come," he said.

"We see if Papa watchin' over us tonight," said Charlotte. She took the peaches and passed them over the soldier's body.

When she finished, Charlotte threw the peaches into the tall grass, disposing of the evil spirits that now clung to the fruit. Then she leaned in close to the beaten soldier. "You hear me, son?" she said.

The man nodded and opened his eyes.

"What your name?" she said.

"Abram." His voice was hardly a whisper.

"Okay, Abram. We gonna take care o' ya, all right?"

He nodded and let his eyes fall shut again.

"Isaac," Charlotte said. "Take this one ta my place. He need rest."

Isaac lifted the man onto his back.

"And be quick," Charlotte said. "There's somethin' on the wind I don't like."

* * *

Captain Seward rode to the front of the company, which had stopped without explanation. "Sergeant Major!" he bellowed.

The clattering of steel rippled through the blackness as Sergeant Major Campbell raced to where Captain Seward sat on his horse.

"Yes, Captain," said the Sergeant Major, out of breath.

"Why are we not moving forward, Sergeant Major?" said the Captain.

The Sergeant Major hesitated.

"Don't stand there like some imbecile. What is keeping us from our duty?" said the Captain.

"The city is a haven for magicks," said the Sergeant Major. "The men are scared."

"Are they sucklings still in need of their Mama's teat?"

119

"No," said the Sergeant Major.

"No!" said Captain Seward. "They are soldiers of the Confederacy. And I want them moving now, or by God, I'll know why not."

"There is another problem," said Sergeant Major Campbell.

Captain Seward could only stare at his Sergeant Major.

"New Orleans is a free city," he said. "We cannot just march in there without provocation."

"Without provocation?" bellowed Captain Seward. "They have my property, and I aim to get it back or receive reparations."

"Yes, Captain," said the Sergeant Major. "But I expect Colonel Radcliffe would relish an opportunity to cite you for insubordination if we circumvented the free city ordinance."

The Captain was silent. He stared across the black fields to New Orleans, torches like pinpricks on the dark canvass.

"We could send in Corporal Butters to parlay with city elders," said the Sergeant Major.

The Captain looked down from his horse, his teeth clenched. "You have one day, Sergeant Major. One day. Then we do it my way."

* * *

Charlotte Lacroix stood off to one side, arms crossed, as Corporal Butters entered the clearing on his horse. Jacques Renaud was at the head of the group, while his brother stood back in the shadows.

"Ho! I speak for Captain John G. Seward of the Second Virginia Army. Who speaks for this crowd?" said the Corporal.

"Jacques Renaud. Constable," said the younger Renaud. "I speak for this group. And what might your name be?"

"That be no need of yours," said the Corporal.

120

"But it be mine," said Charlotte, stepping over to the center of the group. "'Spect you lookin' for that poor man come runnin' in earlier."

"Who might you be?" said the Corporal.

"Charlotte Lacroix. And you be the one needs ta explain how that man come to be as sickly as he is," said Charlotte.

"He's a deserter," said the Corporal. "His health means little to me."

"He may be a deserter, but I don't imagine he signed up hisself," said Charlotte. "'Spect he had nothin' to say in the matter."

"You impudent bitch!" Corporal Butters rose up in his saddle. "How dare you address your betters in that manner."

"New Orleans a free city," said Charlotte. "We don' answer to you."

The Corporal threw one leg over his saddle and made to jump down, but Jacques Renaud stepped between the soldier and Charlotte. "Now, now," he said. "No need for violence. I expect we can all come to some agreement."

"Only agreement the Captain'll grant you is one sees his property returned," said the Corporal.

"She has a point," said Edmand, his soft voice wending through the tiny crowd. "We are a free city."

"What?" Jacques turned on his brother, grabbing the older Renaud by his lapels. "What is wrong with you?"

Charlotte stepped over to the brothers. "Jacques." Her voice was soft but firm as she placed a hand on his shoulder. He turned to look at Charlotte and eased his grip on Edmand. "Don't try to work your magicks on me, witch," he said.

"I do no such thing," said Charlotte. "I put out good causes, good feelings. I no wanna hurt you, Jacques."

Charlotte turned back to the corporal. "That your camp?" she said,

121

pointing past him to the fires along the tree line.

Corporal Butters said nothing.

"I be there in an hour," said Charlotte.

"Not without me," said Jacques.

"You free to go where you want," said Charlotte.

The Corporal nodded in Renaud's direction, then turned his steed and slipped back into the night.

Jacques moved up behind Charlotte. "I hope you don't believe that soldier will be getting out of this city alive," he said.

"We see 'bout that," said Charlotte. "We see. I best go get T.O.M.A.S. Then we head out."

* * *

Captain Seward strode through the tall grass with Corporal Butters at his side. "Well, what do we have here?" he said. "A man of worth and…" His voice trailed off as he eyed Charlotte and the large automaton by her side. T.O.M.A.S. was a collection of gears, springs, and formed sheet metal that resembled a seven-foot-man in the abstract. He (it) was Charlotte's assistant and her confidant – one for which loyalty was never a question.

"Sir," said Corporal Butters. "These are the two who have come to speak on behalf of the city."

"That is quaint," said the Captain. "But I see no reason to negotiate for what is rightly mine."

"Cain't own a man 'ceptin when he wants ta be," said Charlotte, taking a step forward.

"Is that so?" said the Captain. "You are an uppity one."

"Captain," said Jacques. "I believe there is a way for us all to prosper here."

"You do?" said the Captain. "I find that almost humorous."

"You aims ta kill that boy, don't ya?" said Charlotte.

"What?" said the Captain.

"I know what you be," said Charlotte. "How you treat *us*."

"What exactly do you mean?" said the Captain. "What am I?"

"A killer," said Charlotte.

"But isn't that a soldier's job?" said Captain Seward.

"Yes," said Jacques, trying to wedge himself into the conversation.

"I din't know we was the enemy," said Charlotte. "Unless you ain't got the courage ta go North."

Captain Seward stepped right up to Charlotte, his breath hot on her face. "You overstep your bounds," said the Captain, resting a hand on the hilt of his saber.

T.O.M.A.S.'s gears screeched to action beside Charlotte, startling many of the soldiers. The clockwork automaton raised its arms and aimed the miniature steam cannons housed there at the Captain and his corporal. Seward took a step back. "Do you truly believe a single tin man can stand against an entire company of Confederate soldiers?"

"What I believe is that you plan ta kill that boy," said Charlotte. She stared hard at the Captain, as she squeezed the gris-gris in her hand. The small pouch was filled with secret herbs, and it radiated a warmth across Charlotte's palm. The silence built for a long minute before Charlotte finally reached out to T.O.M.A.S. The automaton lowered its arms and powered down.

Captain Seward looked from Charlotte to the clockwork man and back. "You do a disservice to the honor of the uniform I wear," he said. "As much as I might like to be rid of my problem immediately, there are protocols to follow. A deserter may speak on his own behalf. For whatever good it will do."

"That don't reassure me none," said Charlotte.

"I care little about your reassurances," said the Captain. "But," he continued, "You'd be foolish not to consider the persuasive quality of a hundred armed soldiers who would do whatever their captain ordered."

"You plan to kill him, yes?" said Charlotte.

"Will you stop," said Jacques. "That slave belongs to the Captain. It is his, by right, to do with as he wants."

Captain Seward acted as if he didn't hear Jacques. "I expect I will kill him," he said to Charlotte.

"Why you so venomous?" said Charlotte.

"I only want what's mine," he said.

"And then you'll leave us be?" said Charlotte.

Captain Seward nodded, his eyes twinkling in the firelight.

"Let me give the boy some comfort first," said Charlotte.

"If you try to whisk him away, I will bring my company of men down on your head," said Captain Seward.

"We be back at first light," said Charlotte.

"No later," said the captain.

"Don't you worry. You get what's yours come sunup," Charlotte said. Then she turned and, with T.O.M.A.S., headed back across the dark field to the city. Jacques hesitated but soon followed.

None of the soldiers noticed the gris-gris she dropped into one of the campfires as they left.

* * *

"How you feelin?" said Charlotte.

Abram sat up a little straighter on the simple bench in Charlotte's

124

front room. "Better," he said.

"Good," said Charlotte. "Cuz we got some work to do." She opened her front door and motioned for him to join her.

Ten minutes later they returned to the clearing where they first met hours before. A group of citizens, larger than earlier with more women than men, was already gathered – some faces familiar to Abram, ones who had watched Jacques Renaud beat him.

Abram stopped short of the circle, shunning the illumination of the torches.

"What is it?" said Charlotte.

"I won't do this again," he said. "You offered help. This ain't no help."

"These my people," said Charlotte. "You gots nothin' to fear."

Abram refused to move. Charlotte waited before continuing into the circle, where a simple altar became visible beyond the parting crowd.

Charlotte nodded to the darkness beyond the altar. Jacques Renaud was led into the circle by T.O.M.A.S. – the clockwork man's metal arms holding the struggling man with little effort.

Charlotte reached behind the altar and produced a rooster. She turned toward Abram and nodded in his direction. A shiver ran up the man's back, and Abram walked over to the altar.

Charlotte held the bird like a chalice, its red crest a stain of blood in the flickering light, and ran it over Abram's body, drawing away the evil spirits.

Jacques strained against the automaton. "You witch! You'll pay for this! My brother will see to that."

"Your brother done seen to this already," said Charlotte. "You want good, you gotta give good in this world."

125

She turned to the altar and began to chant, raising the chicken high above her head as she prayed in Yoruba to Elegba, Ogun, Obatala, and Oshun. Others joined in, a soft chorus that sailed into the darkness. And then…

Charlotte held the rooster away from her body with one hand and twisted the bird's neck with the other, followed by a second quick motion that ripped its head from its body.

Charlotte dropped the head and held the body above the altar, blood pouring over it all.

Then Charlotte turned and walked to Abram, the decapitated rooster in her left hand. She dipped the middle finger of her right into the neck socket and placed the bloody finger onto the soldier's brow, tracing a line all the way around his head. Dipping the finger again, she knelt down to mark each of Abram's big toes with the rooster's blood.

Charlotte rose, turned on Jacques Renaud, and did the same to him. Renaud struggled, spitting in Charlotte's face multiple times, but he couldn't hope to break from T.O.M.A.S.

When she finished, Charlotte laid the carcass on the altar, offered more prayers to the spirits, then plucked some feathers and scattered them over the altar. Next, she took up a jug of homemade gin – the favored libation of Elegba – sucked deeply from its neck and spattered that across the altar. Charlotte took another long draught of the gin and misted that over Abram's feet and the top of his head. She did the same to Jacques, who continued to struggle as he spat expletives at the voudou priestess.

Charlotte set the gin down and washed her hands in a small bucket off to the side. In the water were floating four coconut shells – divination implements known as obi – which she retrieved and threw. The first throw was black – all four husk side up, Oyekun – a bad omen. She threw them again.

And again. And again. These next three times, they came up ejife – two black and two white – a very good sign. Charlotte was pleased.

She rose and placed the rooster into a small gunnysack in front of the altar. She then poured palm oil and honey into the sack and spit another mouthful of gin over the rooster. Charlotte brought the sack to Abram.

"Seal it," she said.

Then she walked back to the altar and retrieved a small bucket filled with a thick greyish liquid. Charlotte handed it to Abram. "Take this," she said. "You bring it back to my place, where you be staying tonight, and you clean yourself with it. Pour it all over your naked body and don't wash it off until just before dawn. And make sure you throw away that gunnysack on your way back to be rid of them bad spirits."

Abram nodded.

"Now scoot," said Charlotte. She turned and looked at Jacques Renaud. "We got other business to finish here."

* * *

Mist burned off the grasses as Charlotte and her two companions – T.O.M.A.S. and Abram, whose face was hidden by a gunnysack as he struggled against the grip of the clockwork man – approached the soldiers. The sun, a deep orange that burned the eyes, broke over the tree line – *dawn, when the spirits are most restless.* The trio stopped a hundred yards from the edge of the Confederate camp.

Charlotte stepped over to Abram and placed a gris-gris in his shirt pocket as she leaned up and whispered through the gunnysack, "I sorry for this. But to get good you need to give good." She kissed the rough cloth and then turned for the encampment.

Charlotte searched the faces, but did not see Captain Seward. One of

127

the soldiers, working to get his suspenders over his shoulders, locked eyes with her and immediately took off into the woods.

Shortly, Captain Seward arrived in full uniform, clean-shaven, and more alert than any of his company.

"I must admit," he said, "I am mighty surprised." The Captain looked as if he'd just screwed a two-dollar whore and then gotten her to return the money on his way out.

"We all get what we deserve," said Charlotte. "And I 'spect that's as should be."

"That's wiser thinking than I would have given your kind credit for," said Captain Seward.

Charlotte, ignoring the knot forming in her stomach, said, "You be killin' him this morning?"

"If that were your business, I might feel obliged to share," said the Captain. "But…"

He let the word trail off as he turned his attention to the bound refugee in the automaton's steel arms. "I do not mean to cast aspersions," he said, "but might I be able to see the face of that which you brought? Just to make certain this is indeed the one I seek."

Charlotte turned and nodded to T.O.M.A.S. The clockwork man lifted the sack, revealing the bloodied visage of Abram. A thick stitch of cloth was tied around his mouth, stifling protests.

"That be him?" said Charlotte.

"Indeed it is," said Captain Seward. He walked over and punched Abram hard across his face.

Blood trickled from the slave's nose as he pulled his head back up, eyes wide, fear trying to claw its way out.

128

"Corporal Butters!" The young soldier came running, his saber rattling against his leg as he worked to keep his balance through the tall grass. "Yes, sir," he said.

"Take this and prepare for the ceremony. We need to meet up with Captain Jackson's company in Baton Rouge by mid-afternoon, so we haven't much time."

"Yes, sir." The corporal motioned for two soldiers to take the deserter away.

Abram shook his head fiercely, eyes pleading with Charlotte as he disappeared into the forest shadows.

"You best leave now, before I forget my manners," said Captain Seward, and he turned and walked away.

"'Spect you'll hang him," said Charlotte. "'Spect that's right."

* * *

That afternoon, Charlotte Lacroix returned with a handful of others to the soldiers' deserted encampment. She peered into the shadows as she cautiously stepped into the forest. Soon enough, Charlotte found what she was looking for.

The creaking of an oak branch shuddered across the silence, a limp body a pendulum at the end of a thick noose.

"Damn." The muted exclamation came from just over Charlotte's left shoulder. She turned and looked at Abram.

"Yes," she said. "But you give good to get good in this world."

"How will Edmand feel about this?" said another of the group.

"He knows," said Charlotte.

"Yeah, but –"

Charlotte cut off the statement with a searing look that urged the rest of the group back a step. Then she turned back to Jacques Renaud, in a tattered Confederate uniform, hanging above her.

"Someone hoist me up so we'n cut him down," she said.

"Why?" said Abram, the venom obvious in his voice.

"Cuz," said Charlotte, "every man deserve a proper burial."

END

Super Dome

by Jay Wilburn

The river was lapping up over the docks and across the barriers as much from the upheaval of the battle as from the storm still far out beyond the delta. The surf was battering up against the course of the river eating at the shores.

Constable Gravette walked the line with spray soaking and stiffening his leathers. He had long lost his hat and water was running from his damp hair into the collar of his overcoat.

The volunteers were crouched at each post along the lines behind the docks and slips. The band of rain relented and sunlight broke hot through the arms of dark clouds. The patches on the back on the men's battle vests had darkened from green to black with all the moisture. Gravette could still read "The Ignobles" in gold stitching across the crest shaped like the city itself. They held their positions and kept their lids strapped tight in the blazing heat knowing more rain was rotating their way soon.

An explosion out in the broad mouth of the Mississippi brought Gravette's eyes back up even as shrapnel and grit rained down against the brick buildings behind him and as far as the cobble stones in the streets beyond the warehouses. The oaken ship that was belching black smoke from its boiler rolled like a barrel on its brass and bronze ribs across its belly in the angry water. The Allied Colonies of America flag listed with the ship close enough to the independent territory of New Orleans that Gravette could almost count all twenty-six stars and stripes.

He looked down at the Ignoble Militia by his feet. Some of them had working guns. Some of them were loaded. Most were hollow props. A few had the spring loaded Burr Pults which did not require powder and had greater range. They might be able to pierce the wood hull of the Eastern Colonial Empire frigate if it tried to cross the New Orleans line in its desperate death.

Another explosion brought more gritty rain peppering onto the port. Gravette saw it was the ugly metal of one of the ironclads that had been violated this time. It steered away from the frigate and toward the port.

Gravette cursed.

The men lifted their weapons at the sinking ship. There was no chance they would pierce its hull. The submerging vessel would not be deterred by props either.

"Prepare artillery," Gravette ordered.

He heard wheels cranking on the roofs above and behind him. He heard the men groan beneath and in front of him. He knew what concerned them, but to their credit they maintained position.

He could read the casting plate on the ironclad's hull as it steamed forward at the docks. The Free Empire of Western America flashed in the hot sun as it advanced on the neutral port.

He lifted his arm to give the signal and he heard all the men suck in air as they waited.

The constable whispered. "Let history record Gravette's folly as he plunged New Orleans into the East-West War on the opposite end of the Mississippi from the damned Ohio Valley where this useless conflict began."

A few of the men turned their heads when they heard him muttering.

One of the Ignobles pointed at the sky in the direction of the sea. Gravette turned to look and froze. He kept his arm aloft so as not to accidentally send the signal to fire.

The ruddy hull of the zeppelin was torn and flapping as it descended on them. The fabric was folding into the grid work and the skeleton of the vessel was exposed in several spaces. The airship plunged as invisible gas escaped and the vessel was betrayed by its own weight.

"Whose lead balloon are you?" Gravette asked the sky.

He heard one of the men breathe. "Brazil."

They were right. The Brazilian Empire cargo vessel veered toward the water and away from the city. Gravette expected the zeppelin to spear into the FEWA ironclad, but it struck the river ahead of the sinking ship's path. The crew and cargo chamber were under the water before the ironclad crashed and burst through the fragile structure of the downed airship.

The river pulled the pieces out while the rip of the approaching storm cast them up and out of the water again. The ironclad was in the air as it came through. Its propellers spun underneath as it fell back to the water. The ship pitched over itself and raced for the riverbed instead of the shore.

Gravette turned and waved at the roofs. "Belay, all. Hold fire. Hold fire."

"Should we cast lines, Constable?"

"No, we do not pitch aid nor arm to the Ohio Conflict."

As he turned, he saw one man farther up the docks had done just that. Several men cursed as they held position.

Gravette ran along the wharf. Water lapped over the walls and flowed back along the slope into the interior bowl of the city that lay mostly below sea level. Gravette shivered in the heat from the water in his coat and foreboding

133

in his heart.

"Constable? Constable Gravette ... I have a summons from the Regent's Office."

Gravette called back. "It must wait for now. I'm holding off a storm and a war at the moment."

Out in the river the frigate was burning as it sank slowly on its side. Men of the other ironclads were firing on enemies in the water as they pulled up their own soldiers.

"No more lines in the water. Cast no more lines. Pass the word up and down the port."

"The Regent has a message, Constable."

"I said wait. That's my message."

The men pulled someone out of the water that had grasped the single cast rescue line. Gravette reached them as they laid the man out. He was wearing civilian garb and Brazilian colors on his leather apron.

"Thank God ... no more lines. No more lines. Pass the word. Soldiers that make shore should be quartered separately and treated before arrangements are made for return. Slaves will be identified by their brands and then arrested. Do not let them flee into the city before we can arrest and return them. No more lines. If they don't climb out of the water on their own, let them drink. That's the law. That's my order. Pass the word."

"Constable, the Regent ..."

"I said, wait. Now do so before I have you pitched into the river with all of Emperor Edwards' and President Seward's navies."

The messenger stood silently as Gravette pushed the men aside and knelt by the lone crewman of the zeppelin. The man moved his blue lips, but coughed out water instead of words.

134

The sun was swallowed by black clouds in the wind overhead. The temperature dropped at least ten degrees by any system of measure.

"Repeat your words, son. Do you speak English? French? Does anyone here speak Portuguese?"

The crewman's eyes rolled into his head and Gravette thought he was done, but the young man heaved. "My son ... in the cargo hold ... please."

The men looked at the constable, but he would not meet their eyes. "What of the storm? How far off is the storm? How long?"

The crewman began to shake. "Two ... two days out from the city ... no more ... help us, please."

The shaking stopped and the man's eyes slid open blank. The men checked his neck and wrist. Another lowered his ear down to the airman's mouth.

Rain began to drizzle down around them. The ironclads were steaming away from the wreckage upstream. Artillery was sounding from the opposite shore and exploded in the water around the surviving FEWA ships.

"They're not done." Gravette stared out at the water as the drops made circles in the pitching water.

"He is."

Gravette stared down at the body. The rain began to pour down in a wash as the next band of storm arrived.

"Throw him back in."

"Sir?"

Gravette repeated. "Throw him back in. Their ship was involved in the battle even if it was by accident. He stays in the drink unless he climbs out on his own. Pitch him in."

The men lifted the body and carried it out to the side of the dock in the whipping wind and rain. Gravette turned his back without watching them carry out his order.

"Constable Gravette, with respect, you are needed at the Regent's office post haste."

Gravette followed the messenger without making good on his threat to throw him in too.

* * *

One of the servants took Gravette's coat shaking water out of it long after the constable had topped the stairs of the mansion. Water leaked down one wall in a dark swatch and dripped from a discoloration on the ceiling onto one of the statues in the foyer. He pushed his way through the double doors of the office.

The rain battered the tall windows behind Regent Wilkinson's desk, but was then drowned out by the shouting. Wilkinson looked on the constable and then back at the arguing men.

Lightning crackled for the first time outside. The gas lamps around the office dimmed and then flared back to full bright with a drawn hiss.

"Regent, do you want me to arrest someone and lock them in the jail before it floods?"

Wilkinson huffed lifting his head slightly from his hand to speak. "Not just yet, constable, these are the men who are going to save us all, I'm told."

Gravette turned to view the scene more directly. Prints and tools spilled off of the canvas covered tables along two walls. An easel was toppled onto the thick carpet and the display was cast about the floor. There were younger men grouped in two corners watching the exchange as they rolled up plans on long reams of paper.

136

One of the men beat his fist against the table. Spittle dribbled into this beard. The grey, top hat fell away from his head, but he did not try to retrieve it.

The hat struck a model on the table. The model whirled three times. Gravette saw it was a scale of the city. A dozen claws folded up from the perimeter of the model. They locked together in a cover over the city meeting together at curved, riveted seams.

"All I need is the capital, the united manpower, and the airships to set the panels in place." The bearded man bellowed.

The other man swept his hand across the table knocking the dome model onto the floor where the panels clattered apart with the impact. Other models began to whirl and tiny platforms lifted into the air. One clinked off the glass cover of one of the lights and drifted across the room. Another sailed up toward the ceiling and clipped the crown molding with a propeller. A third careened at Gravette's face and he ducked it. If he had still been wearing his hat, it would have speared him like an ironclad in an angry river.

Rain drummed against the window with one turn of the wind.

The second man whipped his head back around between his opponent's clinched fists. His long hair flipped around behind him.

"We must evacuate above the storm."

"You do not escape hurricanes in the air, fool."

"Your panels will break like they did on the floor."

"They are waterproof."

"Water always gets in ... we need to rise above ... I need the ships for the platforms."

"We evacuate and the empires will claim the city in our absence ... in the midst of the storm."

"We will be back before they know."

"We could evacuate up the river if evacuation was an option."

Gravette turned back toward the regent who was watching the exchange calmly.

"Regent?"

Wilkinson turned his eyes without moving his head. He scanned the constable up and down.

"Gravette, you are soaking into my fine carpet. It was laid when my grandfather fled here from the birth pains of the Western Empire."

"It's due to be changed then, Regent."

"Did you manage to keep from plunging us into war, Constable?"

"Barely, sir, but yes."

Wilkinson smiled. "Find some dry clothes. You are so wet your copper badge is going to turn green in front of me."

"It is raining outside."

"That it is, Constable. I'm inclined to settle on the solution of the last man standing. I'll let you carry out the losing argument."

"We have two days before the storm arrives ... maybe less. We need to start moving people up from the lower quarters where the earthen berms might give around the river or high lakes, regent."

Gravette heard the rain so clearly all of a sudden that he actually looked up at the ceiling. One of the models bounced along the flat plaster chipping away the paint. He realized no one was shouting any longer. Gravette looked over and saw the two model makers still and facing him.

The bearded man shook his head. "Two days? Are you certain?"

"How do you know?" the long-haired man demanded.

"A dead man told me when the storm spit him out on our port."

"Where is this man now? We need updated information on the storm to create models and equations to prepare. We must speak with him immediately. Where is he?"

"He just said he was dead, fool."

"He is with his son, but he isn't available for further questioning."

Wilkinson drummed his knuckles on his desk. "We'll need to act now. We must start with the elements of government and the important men of industry ... and their families."

"My dome can save them all. I'll need the airships."

"The ships need to be lifting people not shards of leaking metal."

The argument erupted again and Wilkinson covered his face with both hands.

Gravette turned and walked back along the high banister toward the stairs without being dismissed.

* * *

"Where are the rest?" Gravette shouted over the driving rain.

He pulled the straps tighter on his new hat. It still didn't feel right on his head.

"Some are working with the dome panels. Others are guarding the airships from looters until the regent decides what to do with them, Constable."

"Marvelous ... keep clearing this block. We need everyone to higher ground before the waters rise anymore and the body of the storm sweeps over us."

"This isn't the body of the storm, Constable?"

"Just keep moving people."

"The regent directed most units uptown. What are we still doing down here, Constable?"

"Just keep moving people. Understood?"

"Yes, sir."

Gravette charged up the stairs and beat on the doors of the apartments. "You need to come out. It isn't safe."

"We're on the second floor."

"We've done nothing wrong. Leave us alone, officer."

Some of the occupants came out. They were carrying babies or elderly parents. Gravette left the others and moved to the next building. He called for his men, but they couldn't hear him over the storm. Water was starting to flow through the streets and up over the sidewalks. It was coming from the opposite direction of the sea and the storm.

Gravette squatted down near the gutter and listened. The storm was raging, but he still should have been able to hear it. The gears were silent in the works below the street. He placed his palm on the walk. The water flowed up over his hand and soaked into his sleeve, but he waited. There was no vibration.

He stood and splashed up onto the stoop of the next tenement.

He yelled back. "Work quickly. The pumps are dead under the streets. We're out of time."

Gravette reached the next landing and found the doors to the apartments open. He stepped in and found men tearing drawers out of dressers and cabinets. He just stared.

One of the men looked up and drew a pistol from his belt. Gravette ducked out as the doorframe exploded out in splinters. Another shot burst the trunk pipe across the hall. Steam sprayed out with a high scream. Condensation fell from the ceiling and dripped from the other pipes.

He drew his own weapon as the men shuffled inside the apartment. Gravette backed down the stairs and back out into the storm. The street was washed up to his knees. The current threatened to pull his feet out from under him.

Garrett slogged to the next apartment building. "Anyone? We need to leave soon."

"You need to leave now, Constable."

Gravette held the railing and looked over his shoulder. It was the same messenger from the battle at the port. He was in the seat at the top of the ostrich. The mechanical legs slogged through the rising water splashing up into the air with each step. Water drained through spouts under the bowl of the walker. Mist evacuated from vents under the engine block below the struts connected to the leg joints.

"My men need to be pulled out."

"They should have not still been down here, Constable, but they are being boated out now. Boated out of the streets. You need to come now."

"How many can you fit on that walker?"

"You, Constable, that is from the regent himself."

"There are still people down here. We need to pull them out."

"Why don't you just pitch them, Constable. Those are the orders. They need to pull themselves out at this point. You are ordered to come with me, sir."

"We need to move people. They are our citizens."

"The dome was not placed in time. The airships were not set aloft before the storm hit. One of them drifted into the berms by the lake. We have a breach. Regent Wilkinson needs you to help evacuate VIPs ahead of the storm and the flood."

Gravette turned and ran into the next apartment. He was up ten steps. There were gunshots. The constable turned in time the see the messenger's body float by facedown on the current in the street. He drew his weapon as water sloshed through the open the door and up the bottom steps. The ostrich struggled as the legs fought against the water. Gravette couldn't see who was in the bell of the walker, but he had his suspicions.

"Back in the drink …"

He continued up the stairs and kicked open doors without knocking. "Get to the roof. Get to the roof now."

The families climbed the stairs and pulled down the ladder to the attic. Gravette stopped short at an open door. A small boy was staring up at him.

"Where is your mother, boy?"

He did not answer. Gravette pushed past him and checked every room, but found no one. He came out to find the apartment door open and empty.

He ran back out and found the boy leaning through the wood dowels of the stairwell railing.

"Water."

"Like you don't know, child."

Gravette scooped him up and hauled him up the ladder into the attic. The families were huddled below the heavy beams at the apex of the roof above their heads.

"How do we get outside?"

One of the men said, "This is it."

Gravette carried the boy with him as he scuttled along the floor of the attic. He found the top of one of the trunk, venting pipes. He used the

142

butt of his gun to break through the slats, tar, and shingles. The others joined in and clawed away the broken wood with their fingers until they were bloody. Rain flowed down the pipe and fell in on their heads.

Gravette climbed out first and then had them hand him the boy. He helped pull the others up onto the slippery roof. They used belts and scarves to tie themselves to pipes, hoods, and chimneys.

They could see across the roofs through the quarter where other families had taken to the roofs to escape the rising waters through the streets and alleys. The flood was above the first floors.

A single ship twisted as it rose above the buildings in the distance. The airship fought the wind as it tried to maintain balance with gales pulling at the great platform mounted on it.

Gravette pulled the boy inside his coat as he gripped the vent pipe and watched. The ship careened with the violent wind toward the port. It clipped a single claw of the dome that stood lonely and useless. The platform was damaged, but the twisting ship continued to rise through the storm. The panel wavered and then collapsed into the city. It crashed shaking the ground and crushing dozens of buildings under its metal bulk.

"What's happening?"

Gravette looked down into his coat at the boy's small voice. He looked back into the storm.

"Same thing that always happens, child. Important men fight over bad ideas while everybody else drowns in the middle."

Gravette watched the waters and the escape ship continue to rise. He couldn't decide if he was hoping for the ship to fall or not. He decided to save his hopes for the waters to drop before they swallowed his city.

END

143

The Gift

by Brandon Black

A single hulking form, metallic grey in color, cylindrical in shape, pockmarked with turrets, casemates and firing ports and bristling with aerials, hung high in the morning silence above the horizon. On the bridge of the Texian Air Ship *El Dorado*, Leading Airshipman Wyatt Andersson spied at her using binocular goggles. Wyatt was an able-bodied young man with military regulation length wavy brown hair and a clean-shaven, handsome and youthful face. He was clad in the sky blue shirt and trousers and navy blue cap and neckerchief of a Texian aerial rating.

"She's flying Prusskan colors, sir." Wyatt paused for a moment adjusting his goggles before continuing. "I make her out to be an armored cruiser, the *Brandenburg*."

Zachary Zephyr, captain of TAS *El Dorado*, stood with one foot planted on the raised platform upon which the helmsman's chair was mounted. He stood with one arm braced on his knee and his other hand balled into a fist at his hip; his face shone with a fierce determination that cowed many a lesser man. Zephyr, of course, wore the navy blue jacket, trimmed with gold and the sky blue trousers befitting a Captain of the Texian Air Command, but to it, he added his signature white flying scarf.

Zephyr was a barrel-chested man with a head of hair and a beard the color and disposition of molten fire, hair that somehow always evaded regulation length because no one ever asked. His was a handsome, lantern-jawed visage surmounted with piercing emerald eyes that had bewitched and subjugated the hearts of many a beautiful lady, both allies and enemies. When he spoke, it was with a voice as cool and even as a mountain lake but as solid, rocksteady and reassuring as the mountain itself.

"The Tyrant of Prusska. My guess about his interference with the Peace Conference was right then. No doubt the Prusskans have no intention of our stopping the ambassadors' assassinations without a fight."

Wyatt spoke up again. "She's launching ornithopters, sir." Prusskan *Alder Ritter* ornithopters fell out of the warship's hangar bays in threes, looping back to altitude to form up into arrowhead formations ahead of their mother ship.

Jack Garrison, a lean, muscled, hard fighting man of action with a thin short cropped beard and his immaculate brown hair pulled into a perfectly neat ponytail behind him, was Zephyr's executive officer. Wearing the same navy blue, gold and sky blue of his commanding officer, he was also equipped with a long-range monocular, which he wore strapped over his right eye Garrison turned to his captain and asked, "Your orders, sir?"

Zephyr smiled. "All decks – stand by for action! White Lions are GO!"

"Yes, sir!" was Garrison's immediate and enthusiastic reply. Garrison flipped a toggle at the console before him and the klaxon sounded throughout the body of the mighty warrior airship. He pulled forward the speaking tube leading to the pilots' ready room. "ENEMY ORNITHOPTERS – ALL PILOTS REPORT TO THE FLIGHT DECK – ALL PILOTS REPORT TO THE FLIGHT DECK!!"

Moments later, rapid footfalls echoed from the airship decks, growing louder and louder as the pilots and airship crew raced through the corridors. The White Lions were an exclusive elite, the cream of the Texian Air Command's crack fighter 'thopter pilots and they knew it. In a fight, each one of them was worth at least three lesser men, be it in the air or in a barroom or brothel brawl and every man jack of them would have died screaming in the service of their beloved Texas or if it meant saving Zachary's life. Texian newspapers referred to them as "the Invincible Men of the Sky."

Wings fluttering, the last of the White Lions' *Warwasp*-class ornithopters lifted free from *El Dorado*'s decks, Garrison reported to his captain. "The White Lions are away, sir."

"Thank you, Garrison."

Wyatt cried out suddenly, "Sir! New contact on the portside! One ornithopter. Hovering."

Garrison himself went to the window and adjusted the lenses of his monocular. "One Prusskan *Tri-Wing*! It's red, sir! Blood red! And there's – a man, a masked man – standing atop it. It must be the pilot. I don't see anyone else. He's just – standing there."

Zephyr nodded grimly. "The Red Kestrel. My old nemesis. I'd thought he'd gone over the falls in Bavaria, but I should have known when we didn't find a body that he'd still be alive. Such a magnificent opponent – bravely issuing a challenge to single combat."

"We're coming into range now, sir. Shall I order the anti-ornithopter batteries to open fire?" Garrison asked.

"Garrison, you knave!" the captain cried. "No! I'll deal with the Red Kestrel – alone!"

"Oh Zach!" cried Jasmine Faithe, Zephyr's official biographer, a

146

civilian. Jasmine was lithe yet buxom with long, curly blonde locks, that flowed in ringlets to her shoulders. Her clear, shining blue eyes never left Zachary when he was in the room.

Zephyr delicately placed a hand under Jasmine's chin. "I've got to. The White Lions are the best 'thopter pilots Air Command has to offer, but even they'll have their hands full outnumbered three-to-one. An ace like the Kestrel could easily turn the tide unless he's dealt with. Don't worry, Ms. Faithe. We're going to win." He turned to Commander Garrison even as Jasmine blushed. "Prepare my *Hornet Special* for launch!"

Garrison smiled. "She's already hot and ready, sir!"

"We'll clear you a path and then you sink that damnable Prusskan airship!"

"Aye aye sir!"

"Andersson – you're with me!"

Wyatt accompanied his captain as he raced down the corridor to the aft flight deck. His role as captain's yeoman made him an administrative adjutant to the captain but in Zephyr's service, Wyatt performed a number of ancillary duties, such as personal valet, in addition to handling Zephyr's paperwork.

A short run led the two men to *El Dorado's* flight deck. Wyatt assisted Zephyr in changing out of his jacket and boots and into his pressurized flight suit and parachute. The deck was vacant of fighter 'thopters, save one, Zephyr's *Hornet Special*, a far more expensive and capable craft than the *Warwasps* the rest of the White Lions flew. The *Warwasps* themselves were a cut above the standard *Yellowjacket* ornithopters most Texian squadrons flew, but the *Hornet Special* was a thing of rare beauty, capable of flying faster and higher than any other craft built in the Americas.

147

Zephyr called out to Chief Petty Officer Irving Carstairs. Carstairs was the master of the flight deck and its repair crews. He personally oversaw all maintenance and resupply of Zephyr's fighter. "How is she, Carstairs?"

Carstairs lifted an arm to the heavens in exultation. "Fully lubricated and ready for action!"

Zephyr tossed a quick two-fingered salute to the man. "What would I do without you, Carstairs?"

Zephyr vaulted into the 'thopter's cockpit and with her lift engine humming and her mighty wings beating to life, ascended from the deck and into the open air to seek out his enemy to do mortal combat.

* * *

The day was perfect, the sun shining brightly in the cerulean blue as the marching band played their way out on to the field. Zephyr stood before Lord Lawrence Pemberton-Smythe, special envoy of Her Majesty's government. Zephyr was absolutely resplendent in his Texian Air Command full dress uniform: navy blue jacket with twin rows of gleaming gold buttons from neck to waist, gold brocade cummerbund and epaulettes, sky blue trousers, navy blue spats with their own gold buttons and black, mirror-polished boots. His over-length hair was capped by his officer's hat in navy blue and gold, his flying goggles atop its brim and around his neck was, as always, his lucky white scarf.

"Congratulations, Captain Zephyr! You've handily turned aside the so-called 'Martian threat' defeating the machinations of both the Tyrant of Prusska and the Empire of New Spain. Both Her Majesty's government and the Texian Alliance owe you a debt of thanks! You captured the Loup Garou, discovered the Tyrant's agent, saved the Peace Conference, captured the pirate airship *Banshee* and brought her villainous crew, the Piranha Girls, to justice!"

"And defeated my arch-nemesis, that mysterious masked Prusskan ornithopter pilot, the Red Kestrel, in single combat," Zephyr reminded him as he looked to the sky wistfully, "although not decisively."

"For these and I'm sure many other equally worthy actions, Her Majesty awards you an honorary commission as a Commodore in Her Royal Air Navy and the Victoria Cross. Congratulations!" Pemberton-Smythe beamed as he pinned the sky blue ribboned medal to Zephyr's chest. Wyatt and the rest of the attending crowd burst into applause. Lord Pemberton-Smythe's voice lowered in volume even as he penitently bowed his head. "Once again, I'd like to extend our most heartfelt apologies for the Piranha Girls' escape after you went through so much trouble to capture them and the *Banshee.*"

"Don't worry yourself a bit, sir. I defeated them once – I can do so again."

"Quite so! Quite so!" Pemberton-Smythe agreed.

Lord Pemberton-Smythe stepped to one side and shook Zephyr's hand as the daguerreotypists all but rushed the podium and set up stands with flash powder to immortalize the scene. Peals of applause continued from the onlookers, as well as declarations of affection, some of them quite unladylike Wyatt thought, from Zephyr's female supporters. Wyatt patted his pocket and waited. The daguerreotyping, the questions from reporters and the shaking hands with dignitaries took some time, but, eventually, it all died down and Zachary caught his eye and motioned him over. Wyatt stood up from where he had been sitting on the bleachers and came over to his captain.

Texian air marines were standing between Zephyr and his party and the remaining crowd, keeping them back and asking them to disperse. Wyatt, in uniform, sifted his way through the onlookers towards the captain. As he reached the line of soldiers, Zephyr's voice boomed out.

"You can let that man through, sergeant. He's with me," Zephyr said, with that oh-so-charming smile.

"Of course, sir," the sergeant said permitting Wyatt to pass. Behind Wyatt, the troopers began to gently push those reticent to leave back further and they began to wander off in twos and threes.

With Zephyr were Commander Garrison, Lord Pemberton-Smythe and Ms. Jasmine Faithe. They were all smiles and pleasant conversation. Wyatt reached into his pocket and handed Zephyr the small box he had been carrying for him.

"There's only one thing that would make this day even more perfect," Zephyr began as he opened the box containing the diamond ring and went down on one knee. Jasmine's face flushed instantly and her hands covered her mouth in emotion. "And that's if you would consent to be my wife, Jasmine dear."

Jasmine began to bounce up and down on her heels and tears poured down from her eyes. "Yes, yes, yes, oh Zachary, of course, yes!"

Zephyr stood and took Jasmine into his arms and they kissed. Wyatt, Garrison and Lord Pemberton-Smythe all applauded as did those last few onlookers who stayed nearby for conversation. At least, the males among them did. Many of the women still present became quite dejected at the sight, with one fainting dead away and the rest storming off in various directions in a mutual huff.

* * *

That night Wyatt set out service for two as Jasmine and the captain were having dinner together in his quarters. The captain certainly liked to talk, in Wyatt's experience all captains did, but Zephyr's tendencies in conversation lent in the direction of making short and not-so-short speeches. However, with Jasmine he seemed to have a genuine rapport and actually seemed to listen more than he spoke and the two discussed all manner of things from where they wanted to live to the matter of children. Wyatt was like a fly on the wall, present and yet invisible, or rather even more-so than usual. As Wyatt refilled their wine glasses after dessert, Zephyr turned to him and spoke.

"I do believe that will be all, Andersson. Tell the cook it was one of his better efforts," he quipped.

Wyatt nodded with a smile, leaving the bottle on the table. "Very good, sir."

Zephyr reached out and took Jasmine's hand. She giggled.

Wyatt went to the hatch providing egress from the captain's quarters, turned to Zephyr and Jasmine and bowed. "Then I'll take my leave. Good night, sir, Miss." Wyatt opened the metal hatch and stepped through it, sealing it behind him.

He sighed with a deep exhalation. Tonight had been little different from other nights the captain had chosen to dine in his quarters instead of at the captain's table. The exception was largely in Wyatt's mind, that he didn't want to make a mistake at dinner on the night the captain proposed. Wyatt stood by the side of the door in case he should be needed. From time to time, particularly when he had guests, the captain would require an additional bottle of wine or another helping of dessert or coffee and as Wyatt's quarters were two decks away – Wyatt merited his own small quarters, complete with speaking tube, as the captain's yeoman – it had become Wyatt's way to remain shortly after dinner, just for safety.

The corridor was empty and silent, save for the low thrumming of the ship's lift engines, and Wyatt grew bored quickly, at least until a soft moaning rolled gently and quietly into the corridor from inside the hatch. Wyatt looked up and down the corridor, seeing no one, and leaned a little closer to the hatch. The sweet, lilting offerings of Ms. Faithe's voice intoxicated him and roused him quickly from his boredom – at least they did until a sudden and thunderous echo began to boom outwards from the captain's quarters, which Wyatt could only surmise to be the fierce pounding of both the wooden bedposts against the metal deckplates of the floor and the headboard against the adjacent metal wall. The metal construction of the airship and the pipes between decks and rooms must have amplified the sound, or least Wyatt so hoped, for Ms. Faithe's sake. The air was suddenly rent with Ms. Faithe's cries of pain and/or pleasure and Wyatt could not help but to blush at them.

The voluminous pounding continued while a hatch down the hall opened and a lieutenant made his way down the corridor, looking over a report attached to a clipboard. He stopped before the captain's quarters, opposite Wyatt as the god-awful racket continued. Wyatt stood at attention, red-faced. The junior officer lowered his clipboard and just stood for a moment, listening. The feminine screechings from within reached a fevered pitch and Wyatt simply glared at the man, who quietly coughed into his fist and then proceeded on his way. After several minutes of cacophonous pounding, both the booming and the caterwauling ceased and some time shortly after that, a loud snoring echoed forth from the hatch into the hall. Deciding he would most likely need to provide no further valet services for the rest of the night, Wyatt hung his head and retired to his own quarters with the intention of clearing away the table just before he served breakfast in the morning.

* * *

After clearing away the plates, glasses and silverware from dinner the night before and setting out breakfast for the captain and Ms. Faithe, Wyatt got settled into doing the captain's paperwork and answering his correspondence. There were the usual forms for resupply – spare parts, uniforms, personal weapons and equipment. There were various items to be set out in the captain's diary, both those Wyatt felt it was safe to just go ahead and schedule himself and those he would have to ask the captain about. And then there were the letters of condolence to families and widows. *El Dorado* suffered the highest peacetime casualty rate of the entire Texian Air Command. She always got the toughest assignments, the worst situations and Zachary Zephyr, at every opportunity, exhorted his men to give their very best for God, Honor and Texas. Time and time again, Air Command would send *El Dorado* into a near-hopeless situation only for Zephyr to reach into his miracle hat and pull out a rabbit. But always, at cost. Hence, the highest casualty rate. While the captain wrote out the letters, signed and sent them, it was up to Wyatt to ferret about the ship interviewing surviving friends and co-workers for personal tidbits the Captain could drop into them. It was the easiest part of Wyatt's job, compared to fetching the captain's meals from the galley, keeping his uniforms spotless and pressed, his quarters tidy, bed made, boots gleaming to mirror perfection, his guns cleaned and reloaded, his parachute repacked, checking in with Carstairs to stay apprised of the maintenance for Zephyr's *Hornet* and the White Lions, and checking in with the XO for those reports he needed to have passed on to the captain, begging the captain for permission to put those things that needed to be done but the captain didn't want to do in his diary and generally being at the captain's beck and call every minute of every hour of every day and by far, it was helping with the condolence letters that Wyatt absolutely hated the most.

153

Having made a few trips about the ship to gain some useful personal characteristics and anecdotes about the fallen for the letters of condolence, Wyatt decided he needed a break and made his way to the nurse's office. Joslyn Morrow was the ship's nurse and one of Wyatt's only two real friends aboard, the other being his fellow Leading Airshipman, Shawn Decker, one of *El Dorado*'s signalmen. Joslyn was also one of only three women aboard. Women were as free as men to join the Air Command but Zephyr's influence and his "old-fashioned chivalric nature" wouldn't allow women to serve in positions that would place them in harm's way. And on *El Dorado*, there was a lot of that.

Wyatt knocked twice on the hatch to the nurse's office. Almost immediately came Joslyn's response. "Enter."

Upon entry to the office, he saw that Shawn was already there, lighting a cigarette. Shawn held it out to Wyatt.

"You look like you need this more than I do," he said.

"Thanks, Shawn," Wyatt said, taking the proffered cigarette and drawing on it deeply.

"Casualty reports?" Joslyn asked.

Wyatt shook his head. "Letters of condolence."

"Sorry," Shawn offered.

"Has to be done and somebody has to do it." Wyatt sighed. "We owe it to them and their families."

Joslyn reached down and withdrew a bottle of whiskey which she set on her desk and poured a drink. She slid the drink across the desk over to Wyatt.

Wyatt shook his head. "I'm still on duty."

"You're the captain's yeoman," Joslyn said. "You're always on duty.

154

You don't drink on duty, you don't drink. Now, shut up and knock it back. Nurse's orders."

Wyatt stood there. "I'll put it in writing if I have to," Joslyn said.

Wyatt decided not to fight her, sat down in front of the desk and downed the whiskey in one gulp.

"Say, I haven't seen ol' Jackie around – bastard owes me money – did something happen to him on the last mission?" Shawn asked.

"No," Wyatt answered. "The one before. We did two foreign missions while you were on leave."

"What happened to him?" Shawn asked.

Joslyn lowered her head. "We were ambushed by emerald smugglers in the jungles of Brazil. He pushed me out of the way and wound up taking forty bullets meant for me."

"Ouch." Shawn winced. "Tough break."

"Yep. Quick though," Wyatt said.

"Quick," Shawn agreed, nodding. "Well – to honor him, you could take forty-one," Shawn said. "You know – shots in the foot, take them over time or something."

"To be honest, I had the same thought myself," Joslyn said. "And then I thought, 'that's *stupid*. I'll just get his name tattooed on my breast or something.'"

Shawn nodded. "Nice."

"I think it's what he would have wanted," Wyatt said.

The speaking tube in sickbay echoed into life. "Doctor Yates, please report to engineering. There's been an accident."

"I better get down there," Joslyn said.

Shawn stood up. "I'd better get up to the bridge. My shift is just

155

about to start."

Joslyn turned to Wyatt. "Why don't you come with me? I might need some help."

"With what?" Wyatt asked.

Joslyn looked around, picked up a medical bag and handed it to Wyatt.

"Heavy lifting?" Joslyn offered.

Wyatt shrugged and accompanied Joslyn to engineering. When they arrived, they found the engineering crew encircling a man lying unconscious on the deck. The captain and the ship's doctor, Dr. Wendell Marcellus Yates, arrived on the scene shortly after Wyatt and Joslyn.

"What happened?" Zephyr asked.

"Petersen's new, sir. He wasn't paying attention near the transverse gearing and one of the gear arms hit him. He went over the railing from up there and fell to the deck."

Doctor Yates put his hand over the man's mouth and then placed his thumb and forefinger against the man's wrist.

"He's dead, Zach."

Wyatt ran over to the fallen man and pushed the doctor out of the way. Yates fell to the deck.

"The man's not breathing son, he's dead." Yates said. Zephyr offered a hand to the doctor, who pulled himself up.

Wyatt opened Petersen's mouth and placed his mouth over it, exhaling deeply. He took a deep breath and exhaled into the man's mouth again and again.

"It's no use," Zephyr said.

The doctor waved aside Joslyn who moved forward to stop Wyatt.

"Let him get it out of his system – at least he'll know everything was tried."

Two breaths later and the fallen rating began to come around. The doctor's face turned bright red and everyone, including the captain, was looking at him.

Nurse Joslyn walked over to Mr. McGillicutty, *El Dorado*'s chief engineer, known to the crew as Cutty, who had in his hands an aetheric interferometer.

Joslyn pointed to the device Cutty was holding. "That's a fairly unusual aetheric reading, wouldn't you say?"

Cutty looked at her, blinked twice and then looked down at the device he was holding. "Yes, yes, I would. I'm surprised a woman would know that."

Joslyn smiled. "It *is* the duty of everyone aboard to educate themselves about such matters."

"Agreed," Cutty said. "But I don't see – "

"An aetheric fluctuation from the lift engines must have affected this man's heart. It's the only logical explanation." Trying to disguise his embarrassment, the doctor simply nodded as Joslyn continued. "Any trained physician would have determined Petersen to have met his maker."

Joslyn turned to Wyatt, offering her hand. "Ironically, Yeoman, it was your complete and total ignorance of medicine that enabled you to save this man's life."

Wyatt took her hand and stood up, nodding and suppressing the urge to smile.

Two engineering ratings helped the fallen man to his feet and began to walk with him to sickbay. The doctor accompanied them.

Zephyr slapped Wyatt on the back, nearly knocking him down. "Well done, Andersson, that's the kind of initiative I like to see in my men – *and* you saved yourself another piece of paperwork – although you'll still have to write out an accident report. Ha ha!!" Zephyr laughed.

"Thank you sir," Wyatt managed as the captain took his leave.

Cutty and the other engineering personnel returned to their duties, leaving Wyatt and Joslyn alone.

Wyatt stepped closer to Joslyn and very quietly said, "And thank you."

Joslyn smiled and patted him twice on the back where the captain had slapped him. Wyatt winced. "You're damned lucky I was around. Old Man Yates would have *never* forgiven you for saving one of his patients like that."

"I owe you one," Wyatt said.

"You can buy me a drink at the next port-of-call," she said.

"You're on."

Joslyn waved and turned to head back up to sickbay when Wyatt called softly after her. "One thing though, how *did* you know that was an anomalous aetheric reading?"

Joslyn shook her head. "Don't you know? Those things *always* say there's an anomaly of *some* kind."

* * *

Moored to a tower at the Algiers Aerodrome, *El Dorado* hung suspended in the quiescence lit by the gentle radiance of morning sunshine. Air Command had decided to send *El Dorado* on a diplomatic tour, to show the flag as it were, and the timing had been scheduled far in advance, although no one bothered to give Zephyr and his crew any advance warning. Air Command made an unusual request of Zephyr – to allow them to use his wedding and honeymoon as part of the diplomatic tour, making use of

Zephyr's personal charisma and notoriety, and in exchange, Air Command would pay for both events. The bigwigs back at Air Command felt it would be a perfect event in the perfect place, as the Free City of New Orleans was already a diplomat's playground. Zephyr acquiesced to the request without complaint and Jasmine, dutifully, acquiesced to Zephyr's.

The black dome and surrounding white spires of the local Jesussite cathedral looking over the town square dominated the city's landscape. The cathedral's archimandrite was going to perform the wedding ceremony herself. *El Dorado*'s crew had been invited, of course, and all but a skeleton crew remained aboard during the ceremony. New Orleans' aerial defense militia, the Greyhawks, volunteered to provide added security for *El Dorado* and the other airships in town for Zephyr's wedding. The Greyhawks were known the world over. For though they were a small force, they were an elite one, known for pirate-hunting, and were responsible for law-enforcement within the city's territorial limits as well as for her defense. As a unit, they were descended from the New Orleans Greys who had volunteered during the Texian Rebellion and had fought at the Battle of the Alamo. *El Dorado* was moored opposite *Cassiopeia*, the third cruiser of New Orleans' famous Battlegroup *Constellation*, named for its light cruisers, *Altair*, *Bellatrix* and *Cassiopeia*. Zephyr considered it an honor to have soldiers of such caliber helping out with *El Dorado*'s security during his wedding and intended to return the Greyhawks' kindness with an aerial exhibition by the White Lions.

Wyatt, like most of the crew, was in line outside the cathedral-basilica waiting to enter. Beside him were Shawn and Joslyn. Greyhawk sailors wearing their grey flap-hats and flying goggles kept the crowd behind barricades which had been set up to provide a perimeter around the church. Attendees were searched, as no firearms were permitted by the guests, only blades. After being allowed to enter past the perimeter, they surmounted the stairs to the building proper. Black robed priestesses of the cathedral-basilica, their heads covered in a long solid cloth down to their shoulders, their eyes draped with a second veil of black lace, stood to either side of the walkway and asperged the attendees using willow branches and rain water.

Within the splendid many-columned structure, along the walls flanking the pews were New Orleans Sky Guards armed with ceremonial pikes and longknives. Hanging from the upper level were the flags of many nations: the blue, white and red with three golden fleurs-de-lis of the Free City of New Orleans, of course, the Texian Alliance, the Atlantean States of America, the Republican States of America, the Empire of New Spain, Spain, the New Gaul Republic, and the United Kingdom of Albion and Avalon. Less conspicuously were the riflemen on the upper level overlooking the ceremony, both Texian marines and Greyhawk naval infantry.

The chamber echoed with a multitude of conversations as attendees entered and were seated. The ushers closed the doors and the chamber began to fall silent. The organ sang into life as music billowed through the great chamber and the remaining conversations ceased. There sounded three loud knocks on the doors to the basilica and the ushers pulled open the great doors. The archimandrite herself, clad in vestments of black and silver, with the silver dove of her faith hanging around her neck, and her black conical veiled *kamilavka* hat entered the vestibule followed by Captain Zephyr and Ms. Faithe.

Zephyr, beaming a perfect and immaculate smile, was wearing his full dress uniform. His chest bristled with the medals and ribbons he'd won during his career as an Texian air officer. Ms. Faithe was every bit the beautiful, demure bride of a war hero everyone expected. Jasmine was clad in an elegant

160

white lace-trimmed gown, with a veil that covered her from face to nearly her waist. A long train behind her was held aloft by two little girls dressed in pink.

The archimandrite, still standing in the vestibule, lifted her hands and spoke. "All rise."

The assembled attendees stood from the pews and faced towards the front of the church.

"Beloved gathered assembly, we are here in the sight of the Father, the Mother and the Christos to consecrate these two people, Zachary and Jasmine, into the sacred mystery of holy wedlock."

One of the attending priestesses handed the archimandrite the two wedding rings. The archimandrite lifted them on high and all assembled bowed their heads reverently. "Christos, by your light, bless and consecrate Zachary and Jasmine in love and with compassion for one another. May these rings be a symbol of their true faith in each other, and always remind them of their love and compassion. We ask this in the name of Yeshua Christos, our Lord."

Those assembled replied, "Amen," as they lifted their heads.

The archimandrite placed the rings upon Zachary and Jasmine's right hands.

Commander Garrison, serving as best man as Zachary's brother could not be in attendance, stepped forward with two large ceremonial crowns and handed them to the archimandrite. She touched Zachary's crown to first his forehead and then Jasmine's and then his again, saying, "The servant of the Elohim, Zachary is crowned to the handmaiden of the Elohim, Jasmine, in the name of the Father and of the Mother and of the Christos, now and forever unto ages of ages. Amen." She placed Zachary's crown upon his head. Turning to Jasmine, she touched her crown to her forehead and then Zachary's and hers again, saying, "The handmaiden of the Elohim, Jasmine is crowned to the servant of the Elohim, Zachary, in the name of the Father and of the Mother and of the Christos, now and forever unto ages and ages. Amen." She placed Jasmine's crown on top of her head.

The archimandrite spoke again, "Let us pray to the Christos."

To which those assembled responded, "Christos have mercy."

"Man is born of woman and so it is meet that in the fullness of time as the wheat doth ripen and lengthen, that he should pass from the hand of his mother to the hand of his wife and helpmate, even as he must some day returneth to the hand of the Great Mother at the end of his days. And as woman, too, is instructed and brought up by her father, so it is meet that in the fullness of time as the fruit doth ripen and swell upon the tree, that a woman should go forth into the world to give birth to a new beginning and a new life with her husband and helpmate, even as she, too, must some day returneth to the hand of the Great Father at the end of her days. O Sovereign Christos, stretch forth your mighty hand and join together your servant, Zachary, and your handmaiden, Jasmine, in the spirit of illumination, for by You is a wife joined to her husband and a husband to his wife. May the light of love live forever in their hearts and in their home. May they have true friends to stand beside them, both in times of gladness and in times of sorrow. And may the light that flows to them, and from them, be in ever greater abundance. For Yours is the dominion, and Yours is the kingdom, and the power, and the glory, of the Father, and of the Mother, and of Your Sovereign Spirit, both now and ever, and unto the ages of ages. Amen."

With a great smile on her face, the archimandrite turned to those assembled and lifting her hands said, "By the Grace of the Elohim, by the light of the Christos, I now, with great joy, happily introduce Zachary and Jasmine as husband and wife. Go forth in peace and serve the light. This sacred

162

mystery of matrimony is complete."

Peals of applause filled the cathedral as Zachary and Jasmine kissed for the first time as husband and wife. Wyatt looked over in Joslyn's direction and smiled silently as she cried. Zachary and Jasmine broke their embrace and waved to the attendees as they made their way down the aisle back to the open doors of the basilica. Waiting there, just beyond the doors, were two rows of Texian officers, their sabers held aloft for Zachary and Jasmine to walk under them.

Following the crowd slowly making their way out of the building, were Wyatt, Shawn and Joslyn. Joslyn was still wiping tears from her eyes with a handkerchief. Just as they were about to exit the doorway and join the celebrants talking aside, Wyatt felt a strong sense of unease, an all-too familiar dread. Casting a cautious eye about surreptitiously, he caught sight of shadows in places where there should be none, movement behind trees and in the park beyond the basilica. He grabbed Shawn and Joslyn by their clothes and roughly pulled them to the side of the line they were previously in, preventing them for leaving the building.

Shawn got as far as "What the – " when dark clouds roiled overhead, casting the once-sunny town square into a pall of shadow. Thunder boomed out of what a moment before was a clear, blue sky and a sudden mist rose and then fell. When the mist retreated, there were bald, black clad men spread in a semi-circle around Zephyr and his party. Few civilians had the sense to flee, most were held fast in fear and confusion as to what was going on. Wyatt pulled Joslyn and Shawn down away from the window onto the floor underneath it.

A voice boomed outside. "Zachary Zephyr – the Black Tsarina sends her regards!"

A fusillade of shots rang out and Shawn and Wyatt both just shook their heads.

"Vampires?" Joslyn asked.

"And warlocks," Wyatt replied.

"Both of whom can't be killed by bullets?" she asked.

Wyatt shook his head. "Both of whom can't be killed by bullets."

The sounds of both Zephyr drawing his saber and his answering shout reached into the deep into the bowels of the cathedral. "Garrison, Texians – to me, to me! Charge!"

A Texian marine lieutenant gave the order to fix bayonets.

A young Greyhawk officer cried, "Sky Guards – Greyhawks! Into battle!" And with that, all the armed soldiers inside the cathedral raced outwards to do battle by Zephyr's side.

The sounds of conflict and carnage filled the great Jesussite cathedral as battle raged right outside its doors. Wyatt gestured over to Shawn with two fingers and Shawn pulled out a pack of cigarettes and handed one each to Wyatt and Joslyn before taking one himself. Wyatt lit a match and lit his cigarette before passing the match to Shawn who lit his own and shook it out before the flame could reach his fingers. He took two long pulls on his cigarette and used it to light Joslyn's before continuing to smoke his own.

Most of the attendees now trapped in the cathedral were cowering behind the pews. Suddenly, one cloak-clad young lady with jet black tresses stood up and with a flourish, cast her cloak aside and withdrew in one deft motion a matched set of longknives. "At last, father, at last the man who ruined you, who ruined our dream will die! Revenge! REVENGE!" And with the last, she began to race forward towards the open door.

"Here we go!" Wyatt flung his cigarette aside and motioned for

Shawn to follow him. Staying low, he crawled up quickly to the edge of the pew and flung himself into the aisle just as the young woman got there and she bowled right over him. Tumbling head over heels to the floor, she looked up at Wyatt in confusion for a moment before Shawn bashed her across the face with a heavy hymnal from the pews. Staying low, the two of them pulled the unconscious woman back under the window where Joslyn was waiting. Shawn gathered up her longknives and placed one on the ground beside Wyatt while Wyatt searched the woman. Finding a belt pocket with a length of cord in it, Wyatt and Shawn began to tie her up.

Wyatt picked up the longknife and tucked it into his belt as he turned to Joslyn. "Give me your handkerchief."

The confused nurse did as she was told and Shawn opened the young woman's mouth and Wyatt stuffed the handkerchief into it.

"Who is she?" Joslyn asked.

"Tatiana von Ravencroft. Her father pioneered the transfer of men's brains into gorilla soldier bodies," Wyatt said.

Joslyn blinked. "He put dead men's brains in gorillas?"

"Those men weren't dead until von Ravencroft cut their skulls open," Shawn said. "Even criminals didn't deserve that. The captain had the castle bombed, while he was still inside it, and managed to get out with himself and Tatiana here alive."

"I don't think she's ever forgiven him for it. Saving her, I mean," Wyatt said.

Shawn ran over and retrieved the girl's cloak, cut a strip from it and tied it tight around her head as a blindfold.

That done, Wyatt motioned towards Shawn for another cigarette.

"All out I'm afraid," Shawn said.

Joslyn extended her cigarette to Wyatt who took a pull off it before handing it to Shawn to do the same. "Much obliged," Wyatt said as the three of them smoked the cigarette in succession and waited for the fighting to die down.

* * *

The sun shone once more. The ground lay littered with black-clad smoldering corpses and fallen soldiers and civilians, both men and women. The vampires and their warlock allies were destroyed or fled and Zephyr and Jasmine were safe. Commander Garrison had been wounded, "Just a scratch," he said and he and the other wounded soldiers had been taken back to the airships for treatment since the local hospitals were swamped with the civilian casualties from the engagement. Joslyn pressganged Wyatt and Shawn and several other able-bodied sailors into assisting her in *El Dorado*'s sickbay.

Bleeding men cried out from the pain of their wounds, or lay unconscious, or dying on the beds of the sickbay. Untrained men like Wyatt did what they could to make them comfortable and followed the orders they were given. Medical supplies and trained physicians from civilian airships at the aerodrome were routed to the ships where they could do the most good. The pistons, bladders and billows of steam-driven respirators rose and fell as they assisted the breathing of those wounded who needed it. Wyatt and Shawn lifted the wounded onto beds, held them down as doctors and nurses ordered and gave soldiers liquor to deaden the pain. They also pulled the sheets over the heads of those of them that died.

Dr. Yates entered the sickbay wearing a fancy dinner jacket and formal attire. "Nurse – what the devil's going on? And who the hell are these people treating patients in *my* sickbay?"

Joslyn was cauterizing the stump of a marine's leg that had just been removed while two orderlies held the man down. The sound of his sizzling flesh merged with his screams as smoke curled from his wound and the smell of burning meat blended with the existing aromas of blood, oil, vomit and urine.

"There was an attempt on the captain's life, Doctor. A call was put out to the other airships for aid."

Checking to see if what the interlopers in his sickbay were doing met with his approval and then seeing what Joslyn was doing and the difficulty she was having doing it, Yates asked in an angry voice, "Why hasn't this man been chloroformed?"

"We've run out of chloroform, Doctor. There's some laudanum on its way, but until it arrives, all we have is whiskey," Joslyn responded and finished attending to her patient.

Yates nodded, removed his jacket and went to the sink to wash his hands. The speaking tubes all over the ship echoed at once. "The captain and his wife have been safely brought aboard." A cheer rose up from every deck of *El Dorado* in celebration and relief. Wyatt looked around the room. *All the blood, all the suffering, all the pain, and they still loved him*, he thought. *They'd do anything for him. Anything at all. Because he's their hero.* And, Wyatt thought, *they were his. They were all his heroes because they were common, ordinary men called upon to do uncommon, strange and extraordinary things. And he resolved, then and there, that he would do absolutely anything to keep another one of them from dying from it.*

Yates and most everyone else in the room had lifted their eyes to the speaking tubes when the message sounded and when it ended, they lowered them again. Yates' eyes fell on Wyatt as he turned from the sink and Yates began to angrily stomp in Wyatt's direction. He just managed to get his mouth open when Joslyn cut him off.

"Doctor – have you seen the captain? I haven't seen him come down to sickbay and I'm sure he'd been wounded in the struggle."

Yates nodded with a wry smile. "Airship captains – always thinking they're invincible. I better go up and have a look at him. Make sure the missus is all right as well. You can handle things down here, can't you?"

Joslyn nodded once. "Of course, doctor. If there's something we can't handle, we'll just call."

"Good, good." Yates said and headed off to the bridge.

Wyatt exhaled in relief and turned to Joslyn who flashed a quick smile at him as she wiped her brow with her sleeve and then got back to work.

* * *

The captain's wedding reception was a considerably more private affair than the wedding, particularly after the attempt on his life. While the entire crew of TAS *El Dorado* had been invited to the captain's wedding, the reception was a much smaller happening in a private hotel and open only to a few officers and the personal friends and family of the bride and groom, and, of course, the local diplomats. The attack by the Black Tsarina's forces outside the Jesussite cathedral-basilica caused many casualties and necessitated the canceling of the originally planned reception. Which meant that a new one had to be arranged and orchestrated and, somehow, that duty fell onto the shoulders of the captain's yeoman. Wyatt arranged for a four star hotel down in the Gaulish Quarter that was willing to have the reception, so long as it were held in a curious combination of quiet discretion and heavy security. Fortunately, Air Command was still willing to pay the rather steep fees requested by the hotel for this second reception. With few contacts in the city of his own and those of the local diplomats gone skittish after the attack, Wyatt had to call upon his fellow sailors a little more than he wanted, but in

168

the end, a fine reception was had. The solution to the problem had apparently been to have large quantities of alcohol on hand for those brave enough to attend and so fortunately, it all worked out.

The gifts bestowed upon Jasmine and Zachary Zephyr on this, the occasion of their nuptials, were splendid, eccentric and numerous. Zachary Zephyr was a man of means, being heir to the Zephyr fortune before he joined Air Command but since then, his exploits had become legendary and as the beloved darling of Air Command and the savior of so many, there were diplomats, businessmen and dignitaries from all over the continent and beyond who sought his attention and favor. Jasmine was thus showered with gifts; necklaces, broaches and other jewelry, sculptures and paintings, rare furs and other clothing, furniture and clockwork automatons designed to do everything from assist her with cooking to dressing her in the morning. Zachary was likewise endowed with the rarest and highest quality weapons and fine suits. One diplomat from far Africa even delivered to Zephyr the full body of a stuffed lion. It befell Wyatt, of course, to catalog these and prepare them for transport aboard *El Dorado*.

By far, the oddest piece of the happy couple's mountain of wedding gifts was an ancient sculpture, a totem of some kind from the time when the Greeks knew the continent of North America as Atlantis, an asymmetrical piece of carved stone, covered in runes and strange swirled symbols with flowing, rising spires and sunken, hidden depths. The piece was bizarre, heavy, unwieldy and to Wyatt, thoroughly unnerving. He had heard stories of left over artifacts from Atlantis and Lemuria that were still dangerous in modern times and while he was not a superstitious man, nor one given to gossiping with his fellow Texian sailors, he *had* just seen a battle involving vampires and warlocks on the steps of a church only two days before.

169

There was just something about the piece – something that drew the eye in and down the deep recesses of its surface, across, along and within curves and ellipses that just did not seem to be *so*, as if what he were looking at were not only impossible to fashion with human hands but that it was suffused with an unlikeliness of having existed at all. Realizing he was tired, Wyatt shook his head and regained his focus on his task. His job was to catalog the captain's gifts; he was neither hired for nor qualified to provide an artistic critique of them. Had the gift been made to him, he would just as likely have sold it immediately or even dropped it off the edge of the airship but it had not and so he wrote down the description "stone sculpture from antiquity," a registry number and saw the men mount it on a wooden pallet for shipment and was done with it.

Likewise, the other articles of friendship and adulation received by the newlyweds Wyatt dutifully documented and had placed in crates stuffed with straw and cotton for shipment back to Texas in *El Dorado*'s cargo hold. He took the liberty of asking Commander Garrison to post a guard on the gifts twenty-four hours a day and Garrison happily agreed, referring the matter to the ship's marines. Exhausted but happy to know that his immediate duties of the past few days were finally complete, Wyatt made his way down to his quarters.

Wyatt barely managed to get the hatch open before collapsing onto his bunk. The fact that his face was resting on papers that lay between him and his pillow alerted him to the fact that there was something on his bunk. The top page was a note from the captain thanking him for a job well done and telling him he had earned a three-day pass for his efforts. The bottom page was the pass, left blank other than the captain's signature.

* * *

The next day, the killings began.

When Wyatt ran down to the sickbay, he found Joslyn crying and being comforted by the captain. Doctor Yates stood waiting with a sorrowful expression on his face before a shrouded form on one of the sickbay beds.

"I'm sorry, son," was all the doctor said.

Joslyn stood up from where she had been sitting and flung herself into Wyatt's arms. Wyatt held her, saying nothing. Joslyn's sobs slowly subsided and the captain took her from Wyatt and helped her sit back down.

Wyatt approached the white sheet shrouded form of his best friend.

"Can I see him?"

"He's not a pretty sight," Yates started to say, "perhaps it would be best to... "

"Can I see him?" Wyatt insisted.

The doctor simply nodded and pulled back the sheet. Shawn's face was a frozen mask of terror. His throat had been sliced open as with a razor and cuts and stab wounds were visible all over his chest.

"He was attacked with some form of serrated blade," Yates dutifully reported, "extremely sharp. He suffered multiple severe lacerations and several deep stab wounds. The primary cause of death was his throat being cut." It was obvious to all that the doctor rattled off Shawn's condition simply because there was nothing else to say. "I'm sorry, son," Yates repeated.

"I'm sorry about your friend, Andersson. I can only imagine the assassin was after me and poor Decker got in the way. He was found outside my cabin," the captain said.

"Why was he outside your cabin?" Wyatt asked.

The captain hesitated before responding, something Wyatt had never seen him do before. "I – asked Decker to take over your duties, temporarily, as

171

my yeoman while you were on leave."

"It should have been me," Wyatt said. "My best friend got himself killed cause I was on vacation."

"You can't blame yourself for this son. There was an assassin aboard and Decker ran into him. It could have happened anywhere," Zephyr said.

"*Was* an assassin aboard. Not *is* an assassin aboard?" Wyatt inquired.

"I'm assuming not," Lieutenant Elliot, head of the ship's marines, responded. "My marines have been combing the ship since this happened and have found nothing. Since Decker's body was found in such a prominent place, I'm assuming the assassin was discovered, attacked Decker to silence him and then fled the ship." Elliot paused as if gathering himself up to continue. "I've made my recommendation to the captain that we leave New Orleans at once."

Wyatt looked to the captain.

"If Elliot is right and the assassin is no longer on the ship, then he's in the city. We don't have the means to search the whole city nor do we have a description of the assassin if we did. If the murderer is gone, then the best thing we can do is step up our security and proceed to our next port of call, Atlanta."

"What about Shawn?" Wyatt asked.

"We'll give him a proper military burial at sea over the Gulf and then turn inland towards the Atlantean States."

Wyatt nodded.

"Thank you, sir," was all he could manage.

* * *

They found Carstairs' body draped over the captain's ornithopter. The craft was covered in his blood. Like Shawn, Carstairs had obviously been attacked by someone wielding a serrated metal blade and like Shawn, Carstairs had died without getting out a cry of alarm or leaving any hint of who his attacker was.

The deaths continued. The ship's cook turned up dead. The head of the marines went missing. Every few days, a man would be found dead. The crew started referring to 'the Phantom,' a practice the captain and the ship's officers immediately tried to stem but could not stop. Commander Garrison pronounced the whole thing to be loose drunken airshipman talk and sent out the ship's marines to round up any liquor or hidden stills aboard the airship but everyone saw the measure for what it was: a desperate hope to stem the tide of terror and futility from destroying the ship's morale any further. The simple truth was that there was an assassin aboard and no amount of searching by the crew or the marines seemed to turn up neither hide nor hair of who – or what – was responsible.

* * *

Commander Garrison, manning the bridge on the night watch, stepped out from the bridge onto the deck, made his way to the prow and scanned the horizon with his monocular. One of the latest theories was that the assassin wasn't aboard ship all the time, that some how the assassin was boarding and leaving *El Dorado*, perhaps via a silenced ornithopter. A petty officer called out to Garrison that the captain wished to speak to him and Garrison turned to make his way back to the bridge. At the corner of his perception, however, something shifted. He held his position and did his best to look as though he hadn't noticed. Making the best guess as to where in the shadows 'it' was, Garrison whirled and produced his twin revolvers.

"Step into the light or I'll open fire!" he shouted.

Something in the darkness rolled to one side and Garrison fired twice from both his revolvers. An unknown form fell backwards over the railing of

173

the airship and out into open air.

Armed marines ran to Garrison immediately.

"I think I got the bastard! Yes, yes, I'm sure of it," he said.

Garrison and the marines looked down over the railing at the lower hull of the airship and, certainly, there was no one there.

* * *

The mood aboard ship improved dramatically after Commander Garrison's reporting that he killed 'the Phantom.' That there hadn't been any further murders put the crew's mind to rest. It certainly improved Wyatt's morale to no end. Wyatt lay awake in his bunk in the dark recalling the past two weeks' events, particularly the death and funeral of his friend, Shawn. He lay there, staring upwards into the darkness of the unlit room trying to make sense of all that happened.

It was there, he thought. There was a thread of connection, some common element that his conscious mind missed but he could feel it was there. Shawn was murdered outside the captain's quarters. Carstairs was murdered while working on the captain's ornithopter. So the captain was an obvious connecting thread. He was the only target of note aboard the ship anyway. *So was someone trying to eliminate those closest to the captain?* Shawn had been killed while serving in Wyatt's capacity as the captain's yeoman. If the assassin thought his death would rattle the captain, he was wrong. But someone who didn't know Zephyr certainly could have thought that killing those around him might break his resolve. Wyatt was thankful Ms. Faithe, now Mrs. Zephyr, left the ship back in Atlanta.

Commander Garrison was the ship's XO and the captain's closest friend, and so again, the captain seemed a connecting thread. But that left the other murders. The ship's cook bore no close connection to the captain and the marine lieutenant was just one of the ship's junior officers. He had no close connection to the captain at all.

Wyatt snapped his fingers as the answer sprang into clarity in his mind. *The captain wasn't the connecting thread! It was the captain's voice!* Shawn would have knocked and asked for permission to enter the captain's quarters or would have been given leave to depart by the captain if withdrawing from them. Carstairs would have reported in to the captain or been queried by him regarding the status of his ornithopter. Garrison was being called to speak to the captain when he was attacked. The ship's cook was always getting special requests directly from the captain and the captain certainly would have been conferring closely with the marine lieutenant with the assassin aboard. *The speaking tubes!*

It had to be the speaking tubes! Someone – something – was hunting the captain by sound! But what? Some sort of automaton? Some device that some enemy of the captain smuggled aboard that was trying to localize his whereabouts by the sound of his voice and the speaking tubes were both leading it towards the captain and confusing it. The tubes went throughout the whole of the ship and the captain could use them any time he wanted to call for an officer or enlisted man or query the bridge's status or some such. *The clockwork assassin was chasing echoes throughout El Dorado trying to find it's prey!*

"Andersson, could you bring those resupply papers back up to my cabin? I think I might have missed something." The captain's voice floated out of the speaking tube in Wyatt's quarters and he froze.

Reaching over slowly to his left, he picked up a match and struck it against the nightstand fully expecting to see an eight-armed, blade-wielding clockwork arachnid of death hanging on the ceiling above him. The match sputtered into life, casting a flickering light throughout the cabin.

175

Above Wyatt, in a corner of the small stateroom was a tattooed brown-skinned Pygmy girl, a serrated knife in her hand and cataracts covering her eyes. She sprung downwards towards Wyatt in his bed, knife poised to stab him.

Confused and alarmed, Wyatt rolled out of the bed as the Pygmy girl crashed into his bunk. The match went out instantly. Wyatt swiped at the nightstand, hurling the unlit oil lamp forward into the night in the vague direction of his attacker. He could hear it smash against the wall. Pulling open the drawer of the nightstand, he fumbled inside for his lighter and managed to roll away from the nightstand as a form brushed him in the darkness. Wyatt winced in pain as the edge of her knife grazed his upper arm near the shoulder.

With his left hand, Wyatt flicked open the lighter as he found himself in a crouched position. By the pale light he could see his attacker likewise crouching on the bunk, preparing to spring at him again. Silently, Wyatt cursed that his revolver was under his pillow. Holding his breath and spying his pen and notebook on the desk, he lifted up the notebook and tossed it over to one side of the Pygmy. The girl's head turned instantly towards the sound but she made no other movement. Wyatt dropped the lit lighter onto the papers on his desk. They immediately burst into flames. Wyatt then jumped towards the bookshelf and knocked over some of the books, jumping back towards the desk as the Pygmy all but flew through the air to crash into the bookshelf. Wyatt grabbed the wooden chair under the desk and when she pounced in his direction again, knife drawn, he swung the chair at her as hard as he could. The impact sent the Pygmy girl reeling into the corner where she slumped into a heap and did not move. Her blade had come free from her hand and was on the floor next to her.

176

Wyatt looked for a second towards the growing fire on his desk and decided to leave it for the time being. He kicked the knife away from his assailant and grabbing his bedsheets, scooped up the unconscious form of the Pygmy girl and tied her up in the bedsheets like a child in a papoose. That done, he snatched up the pillow from his bunk and beat out the fire on his desk. Tearing loose part of the pillow case, he made an impromptu bandage to stop the bleeding from the cut on his arm.

Exhausted and still quite confused, Wyatt picked up the Pygmy's knife and his revolver and tucked them into his belt. Making sure his captive was bound tightly about her person with the bedsheets, he flung her over his shoulder and made his way to the captain's quarters.

Wyatt's fellow crewmen in the corridors looked on in astonishment as Wyatt carried his burden to the captain's chambers with a determination that caused no one to question him as he made his way. He knocked on the captain's hatch.

"Permission to enter," Wyatt said.

"Enter," came the captain's reply.

Wyatt cycled the hatch with his right hand while he held onto his burden with the left.

"Now what can I do for you – " the captain started to say as Wyatt unceremoniously flung his captive onto the sofa.

Both Captain Zephyr and Commander Garrison looked on in a state of amazement at the unconscious girl on the captain's sofa.

"Andersson, is there some reason you're carrying an unconscious Pygmy around my airship?" the captain asked.

"This – " Wyatt gestured to his prisoner, "is the Phantom, gentlemen."

177

"I think you better explain please, Andersson," Zephyr said.

"Of course, sir," Wyatt said. "She was hunting you by sound. Every time you used the ship's speaking tubes, she was trying to gain a fix on where you were so she could kill you. But the tubes kept throwing her off. I had worked it out just as you'd asked me for those papers and I guess from your previous messages to me in my quarters, she had decided that was a place you might be. Luckily for me, I got the better of her."

Garrison stuck his head out of the hatch and looking at the growing crowd gathering there told someone to fetch the marines.

Wyatt looked confused for a moment. "I thought it was an automaton. I figured someone had smuggled aboard a clockwork that was hunting you by sound. The only thing I can't figure out is – who in the world would send a blind dwarf assassin to kill you?"

Zephyr and Garrison looked at each other. "Mendrygal."

"Who?" Wyatt asked.

"Dr. Grigori Mendrygal," Garrison said. "He's been trying to kill Zach for years. He probably grew her in one of those wretched laboratories of his."

Two marines entered the cabin and Garrison turned from Andersson to his captain. "So what do we do with her?"

Wyatt spoke up instantly. "I have a few ideas. Starting with, let's just drop her off the edge of the airship."

Zephyr and Garrison looked to each other before turning back to Wyatt.

"What?" Wyatt said. "She killed Shawn. She killed Carstairs. She tried to kill the commander and me and it was only a matter of time before she tried to kill you too, captain."

Zephyr simply shook his head. "We can't do that."

"She killed Shawn," Wyatt repeated.

"And she'll be executed for it – after a fair trial," Zephyr said. "But we are Texians – if you say to me that your honor won't permit you not to see justice done with your own hands, then I won't interfere."

Wyatt looked to the unconscious girl bound in sheets and then to the floor. "No. That won't be necessary, sir."

"Good. I'm glad. You've done very good work here Andersson. As always. Name your reward. If it's in my power to grant, you've got it," the captain said.

* * *

Wyatt was packing the last of his clothes into a trunk. His books and other possessions were in boxes around his quarters awaiting his departure.

Joslyn leaned against the bulkhead as Wyatt packed. "So you asked for a transfer?"

"In a manner of speaking," Wyatt said. "I asked for his letter of recommendation for promotion to midshipman. Do you know what he told me?"

"What?"

"He told me 'write it out and I'll sign it for you.'"

Joslyn smiled. "Cheeky bastard."

Wyatt and Joslyn laughed.

END

Kilkarney's Map

by Gary Bourgeois

"I've come to you, sir, because you are widely regarded as the best at what you do. There is no finer cartographer on the Gulf Coast, indeed, perhaps in all of North America."

In his lilting Irish brogue the speaker had introduced himself as Errol Kilkarney. He was a large man, over six feet tall and, although not fat, of substantial girth. He had a fair complexion, reddish blond hair, lively green eyes, and a ready smile. His expensive suit and silver-headed cane bespoke a gentleman of some means.

While Kilkarney was certainly charming, he was also quite correct. My father, Theodosius J. Theriot, was indisputably the most respected producer of maps and charts in the region. Almost everyone who sailed on, or flew above, the Gulf of Mexico, the Caribbean Sea, and the surrounding lands and islands had a set of charts from our riverfront shop. Father owed his success to the fact that he was very good at what he did, and because he came into the field about the same time that airship flight was becoming common. The advent of steam-powered, lighter-than-air flight had made it possible for maps to be produced with theretofore unknown detail and fidelity, while creating a nearly insatiable demand for accurate topographical maps of the landmasses over which the airships flew.

"You do me great honor, sir," Father replied graciously. "Now, what is it I may do for you?"

"I would like to have a copy made of this map," said Kilkarney, and he handed over a tubular, leather map case.

My father opened the case, took out the map and unrolled it on the desktop. I moved closer to look over his shoulder. The map was approximately eighteen by twenty-four inches and was hand-drawn and painted on parchment. No compass rose was apparent, but given the standard convention to orient maps and charts with north at the top, the map appeared to show the southern coast of a hilly or mountainous landmass, though without any topographical lines. Relative differences in elevation seemed to be indicated by changes in color and tone. A black, Maltese-style cross was drawn inland near the coast. A star in the lower left corner was marked '21°N / 80°W.' From this latitude and longitude reference I surmised the map showed a section of the south coast of the island of Cuba. The other notable feature of the map was an enigmatic notation at the right edge, which read 'twixt the peaks then score the rod half water half rum.'

Over the years we had frequently been asked to copy or produce maps and charts annotated with cryptic symbols and coded messages—usually by eccentric old salts missing a body part or two. Almost all, I'm sure, had been delusions or hoaxes. So Father didn't bat an eye as he said, "Oh yes, Mr. Kilkarney, we'll be able to do this for you, discreetly of course, for, say, twenty-five dollars?"

"A fair price for the workmanship of a craftsman such as yourself," replied Kilkarney.

Father chuckled. "Well, the work on this piece will actually be done by a set of eyes much younger than my own." Indicating me with a wave of his hand, Father said, "My son, Paul, will make the copy for you."

"Ah, the 'son' of 'Theriot and Son,' as it says on the sign outside. And how long, young Mr. Theriot, do you anticipate it taking?"

"I assume you want an exact copy?" I asked.

"As exact as you can make it. Although, a good quality paper may be substituted if parchment is not readily available."

"Would you like me to add contour lines to this section of the coast for you?"

"Oh no," he responded abruptly and emphatically. Then, recovering his composure just as quickly, he added, "Just the way it is, if you please."

"I'd like to have a week to work on it, then. There are several colors and shades involved. I'll need time for one color to dry before applying another."

"That will do splendidly. No rush. I'm staying at the St. Charles Hotel. Will you be able to deliver it to me there when it's ready? Splendid. Then, sirs, I bid you a good day."

* * *

I had apprenticed to my father at the age of twelve and had spent almost all of my available time outside of schoolwork in Father's shop. When I had finished my basic school education I became desirous of seeing the lands and seas I had spent so many laborious hours sketching, coloring, and printing. So, at eighteen, on the pretext of furthering my cartographic abilities, I had asked my father's permission to sign aboard an airship. To my utter delight, agreeing that firsthand experience would indeed make me a better mapmaker, Father had given his assent. I could indulge myself upon my promise to return before my twenty-fourth birthday. For the next five years I had traversed the skies above worlds I had known only on paper.

And at the end of those five years—for all my glorious adventures, for all the wondrous sights I saw, and for all the fascinating people I met on my marvelous voyages—I had been content to come home to my father and our shop of paper and ink. And it was true. Seeing it all firsthand had made me a better mapmaker. And it was this experience, I feel, that first lead me to suspect there was something amiss with Kilkarney's map.

The afternoon of Kilkarney's visit I took his map, cut a sheet of paper to match it, and sat down with my drawing tools to make a first sketch. The map was fairly old—no one uses parchment anymore—but in very good condition. It looked like it had spent all of its life rolled up and locked away. With its cross-marks-the-spot and cryptic riddle, it had the look of a bogus treasure map intended to separate the gullible from their money. And with his easy charm and smooth style I could readily see Kilkarney as a successful confidence man. But, of course, I could be wrong, and Father had a longstanding and wise policy of not inquiring too deeply into our clients' business. I carefully drew in the coastline, marked the locations of the cross and star, and copied the riddle. Looking at what I had done, I got the nagging sensation there was something not quite right about it. I compared my sketch against his original but could find no deviation. The feeling was still there, though, and I couldn't quite put my finger on what was bothering me. By then, it was getting late and time to close the shop. I shrugged off the feeling, placed the original back into its leather case, and placed the case in a cabinet at the back of the shop.

* * *

"Oh, my God."

"Father, what is it?" We had just opened up the morning after Kilkarney's visit. My father had walked about a dozen feet into the shop and

183

stopped stock-still. I stepped up even with him to see what the matter was. Our once neat and orderly shop was a shambles. Maps, charts, and atlases had been pulled from their shelves and lay strewn across the floor. Nearly every desk drawer and cabinet door had been opened and disgorged of their contents.

I pushed past Father and into the back room. The rear door had been forced open. "Whoever it was broke in through the back door," I said as I returned to the main room.

"All the years I've been here nothing like this has ever happened before," my father said in disbelief.

On a sudden impulse I went to the cabinet where I placed Kilkarney's map the evening before. It was gone.

"They've taken Mr. Kilkarney's map," I said.

"Are you sure?"

"Yes, I left it in here when we closed last evening and it's not here now. God knows what else they may have taken."

"It'll take all day to straighten this up."

"Why don't you just have a seat for right now? I'll go find a policeman and then we can see about straightening up." I took a deep breath and let it out. "I'll have to go tell Mr. Kilkarney about his map."

* * *

Kilkarney had rented a suite on the top floor of the St. Charles Hotel and it was with some trepidation that I knocked on the door. The map was obviously important to him and I did not know how he would take its loss. I had located my pencil sketch among the papers on the floor of the shop and I planned to offer the completion of it free of charge, with his help, of course, to fill in the details.

184

On my way to the hotel I had been rehearsing in my head what I would say, but all that planning went out the window when I beheld the large, dark eyes of the young woman who opened the door to the suite. "Uh. . ." was all I was able to manage.

"Yes, sir? May I help you?" She was trying to maintain a straight face, but there was a gleam in her eyes that betrayed her amusement. I didn't blame her; I must have presented a singularly comical sight.

I managed to close my mouth and start again. "Sorry. I'm Paul Theriot. I was hoping to find Mr. Kilkarney."

"Oh, yes, of course, from the map shop. Please come in, Mr. Theriot. My father is in the next room. I'll tell him you're here," she said, inviting me into the suite's sitting room.

Her heart-shaped face was fairer than her father's. Those large eyes were dark brown and her hair was as black and shiny as a raven's wing. She was nearly as tall as me and had some of her father's robustness of build. But where his accent was Irish, hers was Italian.

"Is someone at the door, Carlotta?" Kilkarney's voice could be heard from the next room.

"Yes, Papà, it's Mr. Theriot from the map shop."

Kilkarney hustled into the sitting room in his shirtsleeves with his tie only half done. "Ah, Mr. Theriot, how nice of you to come by. Carlotta, this is Mr. Paul Theriot of 'Theriot and Son.' Mr. Theriot, my daughter Carlotta. Certainly, Mr. Theriot, you haven't finished with the map so soon. You have perhaps a question regarding its execution?"

"No, sir, I'm afraid I've come with bad news. Our shop was broken into last night. Your map has been stolen."

"Oh my, that is distressing news." His reaction was a lot milder then I

185

had anticipated. He glanced over to his daughter and it was plain something was communicated between them. But just what, I could not tell.

"Were there other items stolen along with my map?" he asked.

"We're not sure how much was taken. The thief left the shop in a shambles. Most of our inventory is made up of prints of our most popular maps and charts. I'm afraid we didn't keep an accurate record of our stock. We'll probably never know exactly what else was taken. Nothing like this has ever happened to us before."

"A great pity. You've reported the incident to the police? Do they have any idea who may have done such a thing?"

"Not at this time," I responded. "The police think the maps may have been stolen to be sold somewhere out of town."

"It's a sign of the times we live in I'm afraid. Still, I suppose, there's nothing to be done about it now," he said philosophically.

"Actually, sir, I believe I may be able to do something. Last evening, before we closed the shop, I made a rough sketch of your map. With your assistance in filling in the details I'm sure I can recreate your map. Free of any cost to you, of course. Then, if you'd still like a second copy, I will be happy to do that one for you for the agreed upon price."

He smiled broadly. "I commend your diligence, young sir, and your sense of what's fair. But there is no need, nor time for it."

"Oh?" I was becoming even more perplexed.

"My plans have changed since last we talked. My daughter and I will be leaving New Orleans sooner than we had anticipated." He picked up a copy of a newspaper that lay on a nearby lamp table. I saw that the paper was folded over to the weekly schedule of ship and airship departures. "Perhaps as early as this afternoon," he said with another glance to Carlotta. "But there is something you may do for me, Mr. Theriot. I know this may be a bad time for you and your father, but if you could supply me with the most recent topographical map you have of the island of Cuba, I would be most grateful."

"Uh, yes, we keep quite a few of those in stock. I'm sure I'll be able to find one. Do you wish to pick it up at the shop, or shall I deliver it to you here?"

"We shall have to check out very soon, Papà, if we're going to make an afternoon flight," Carlotta said.

"That's true and we do have one or two items of business to complete before we leave," said Kilkarney.

"Perhaps there's somewhere I can meet you," I offered.

Kilkarney looked again at the departure schedule and then at his pocket watch. "Would you be able to meet me at, say, one o'clock?"

"That should be no trouble. Where would be convenient for you?"

He thought for a moment and then smiled. "I know, how about if we meet under the Captain's ass? Do they still say that in New Orleans? They used to when I lived here."

I was a bit surprised that he used such language in front of his daughter. A quick look in her direction, however, showed her to be more amused than embarrassed. "Uh, yes, sir, some do. I know where you mean. I shall meet you there at one o'clock. It was a pleasure to have met you, Miss Kilkarney," I said, bowing.

"And you as well, Mr. Theriot," said she, executing a demure curtsey.

I left the St. Charles Hotel thoroughly confused. Yesterday, the map had meant enough to Kilkarney to commission an exact copy. Yet, today, he accepted the original's theft with less emotion than my father shows when he misplaces an old sock. Indeed, toward the end of our conversation Kilkarney

187

seemed jovial. Previously, there had been no particular rush to complete a copy of the map and he had been adamantly against adding contour lines. Now, he and his daughter were in a hurry to leave town with the last minute acquisition of a topographical map of what I believed to be the same island. Despairing of being able to figure out what had caused such a drastic sea change, I shook my head and consoled myself with the thought that I might, at least, have another chance to see Carlotta before she and her father left New Orleans.

* * *

Father and I were making good progress getting the shop back in order and it wasn't long before I located one of our large maps of Cuba. Kilkarney's cavalier attitude toward the theft of his map made me curious, and remembering my nagging feeling from yesterday I decided to compare Kilkarney's map to the one of Cuba I had in my hand. I retrieved my pencil sketch and laid both out on my drawing table. Finding the intersection of twenty-one degrees north latitude and eighty degrees west longitude, I located the portion of the island depicted on Kilkarney's map. It was the coastline immediately east of the town of Trinidad. There was no distance scale, however, so it was impossible to tell exactly how far along the coast his map extended. But it was immediately obvious that Kilkarney's map was in error. As you moved along the coast from west to east, his map showed the coastline sloping to the north, where in actuality that section of the coast slopes to the south. A closer examination of the two maps revealed several other discrepancies. Most notably, a prominent spur of land that jutted into the Caribbean some distance southeast of Trinidad was missing entirely from Kilkarney's map.

I had just decided that his map was the product of amateur

carelessness and was in the process of putting it away when something about the coastline to the west of Trinidad caught my eye. Comparing my sketch of Kilkarney's map to that section of the coast, I noticed that one or two features appeared similar, yet still different. With sudden inspiration I retrieved a sheet of tracing paper and traced the coastline of Kilkarney's map in heavy pencil. I then turned the tracing paper over and compared it to the coast west of Trinidad. It matched perfectly. Kilkarney's map was a mirror image of the Cuban coast between the towns of Cienfuegos and Trinidad. Anyone searching for the location indicated by the Maltese cross on the stolen map would be looking in the wrong place. Kilkarney's map was a deliberate deception. And why a deception if there was nothing to find? Could the map actually lead to something of value?

And then something else occurred to me: Was it possible that Kilkarney intended all along for the map to be stolen? To intentionally mislead a rival or competitor? It would certainly go a long way in explaining his change of attitude and plans from one day to the next. And if so, it also meant that he owed my father, at the very least, an apology for all the time, money, and aggravation this burglary had cost us. I fully intended to ask Mr. Kilkarney some very pointed questions when we met that afternoon.

* * *

Steam carriages and tractors competed with horse-drawn landaus and freight wagons pulled by mules for space on the street outside our shop. Yapping dogs and ragged children darted haphazardly through the heavy traffic, eliciting occasional invectives from overstressed drivers. Over the levee on the riverfront, tall steam-powered cranes and burly longshoremen offloaded and loaded cargo from filigreed riverboats and iron-hulled ocean traders. Smaller service vessels, many still propelled by oars and sails, shuttled among

189

the dozens of ships and boats riding at anchor waiting for their turns at the busy wharves.

Located between the river and the triad of the Cabildo, St. Louis Cathedral, and the Presbytere, Lafitte Square was just a few minutes' walk from our shop. The square was named for Jean Lafitte, hero of the Battle of New Orleans, the last major naval battle fought exclusively by sail-powered, surface ships. Tree-lined, lushly landscaped, and flanked by shops and restaurants, the square and its surrounding buildings were the center of municipal, ecclesiastical, and social life in the city.

I arrived there a few minutes before one and, as was usual for that time of day, the square was filled with people of various ethnicities, nationalities, and languages. A bronze statue of Capt. Lafitte stood atop a marble pedestal at the center of the square. Arms crossed, spyglass and pistol in either hand, the captain stood gazing sternly to the northeast, toward Lake Borgne where he had ambushed and defeated a British invasion fleet over forty years ago. With the map of Cuba rolled and tucked under my arm, I made my way through pedestrians and leisure-takers to the backside of the statue to await Kilkarney.

I didn't have long to wait. I was checking my pocket watch against the time on the cathedral's tower clock when I heard him call my name. He was approaching at a brisk walk, a broad smile on his face. I did not see Carlotta with him.

"Mr. Theriot, I see you're quite …" We were just a few feet away from each other when the sharp crack of a pistol shot was heard from very close by. Kilkarney lurched forward into my arms, taking both of us to the ground. People near the shooting screamed and uttered oaths of surprise and shock. As I was going down I had a brief glimpse of a bushy-bearded man in

190

a wide-brimmed hat turning and running away through the stunned crowd. I landed on my backside with Kilkarney's head in my lap.

He looked up at me, smiled weakly, and wheezed, "Cross . . . and double-cross." He coughed and then convulsed.

I tried to provide support for his head. "Don't try to talk, sir. Help will be here soon."

But it was too late. Blood trickling from the corner of his mouth, he whispered, "Carlotta." Then his body went limp and his once bright eyes dimmed. Errol Kilkarney had died in my arms.

* * *

I didn't sleep well the night following the shooting. Aside from the shock of the killing itself, I found that my feelings for the Kilkarneys were conflicted. In spite of my early suspicions I had liked Kilkarney and I definitely had been attracted to Carlotta. But Kilkarney's last words confirmed he had been running some sort of scam involving his deceptive map, a scam that had involved my father and me without our knowledge and certainly without our consent. And even if she wasn't directly involved, I was sure Carlotta had known what her father had been up to. Now Kilkarney was dead and Carlotta was missing.

The police wanted Carlotta's help to identify the bushy-bearded man I had seen running away from the scene of the murder. They had looked for her at all of the depots for departing passengers, but there was no sign of her. She hadn't gone back to the St. Charles Hotel and her name hadn't appeared on any of the passenger lists for vessels that had already left the city. It was quite possible, of course, that she had left New Orleans under an assumed name, or on a vessel that required no names. I found it difficult to believe that she would have left her father's body behind, unless she was in grave danger herself. Despite her obvious complicity in her father's scheme, I was still concerned for her safety.

As to the particulars of Kilkarney's scam, that mystery deepened with the first visitor to our shop the next morning.

"Good morning, gentlemen. My name is Quentin McCoy, with Commercial Bank of New Orleans. I'm looking for Mr. Paul Theriot."

"I'm Paul Theriot, Mr. McCoy. What can I do for you?"

"I have instructions, sir, to give this to you first thing this morning." McCoy handed me an envelope. "And to wait and inquire if the amount will be sufficient."

I opened the envelope and took out a handwritten note. "It's from Mr. Kilkarney," I said in amazement.

"What does it say?" Father asked, moving closer.

"It says, 'Sorry to be the source of so much trouble. Want you to know that it was all in a good cause. Apologies, Errol Kilkarney.'"

"And the amount, sir? In the envelope," Mr. McCoy prompted.

I looked in the envelope again and took out two crisp, one hundred dollar bills. I was stunned. "Yes, Mr. McCoy, I'm sure this will be sufficient. And, if I may ask, when did you see Mr. Kilkarney?"

"Less than an hour before the poor man was shot and killed," he said, shaking his head. "I may have been the last person he talked to before he died. It's shocking, quite shocking, indeed, to have murder committed in a public square, nearly at the doorstep of the cathedral, and in broad daylight. I tell you, gentlemen, the criminals are getting more brazen every year. It will be this city's ultimate undoing if the mayor and the chief of police can't get crime under control. Shocking, quite shocking."

"Did Mr. Kilkarney give any indication of what his business was in

New Orleans?" I asked.

"All Commercial Bank did was handle the telegraphed transfer of some overseas funds for Mr. Kilkarney — I'm not at liberty to say from where, you understand—and to open up an account for his use during his stay. It's quite a convenience for our international visitors. As for anything else, we at the bank make it a practice not to inquire too deeply into our clients' affairs."

"No, of course, not," I said.

"There is a tidy sum of money left in his account, by the way. I understand his daughter had been traveling with him. She'll be able to access the account—once the proper paperwork has been filed, of course. I've heard she's gone missing, though. It would be dreadful if something were to have happened to her, as well," he said somberly. "Well, gentlemen, if you are satisfied with the amount, I shall take my leave. I'll just leave one of my calling cards with you. Commercial Bank would be pleased to have your business. Good day, sirs."

"Well," Father said, after McCoy had gone. "It seems that even after death Mr. Kilkarney is capable of the unexpected."

* * *

It had started raining just before noon; a grey, soaking rain that kept all but a few hardy souls inside. I had busied myself around the shop, running off a couple of print orders and conducting an inventory of our stock. Other than a few items that had been damaged, our inventory did not appear to have been impacted much at all by the break-in. It was very likely that nothing other than Kilkarney's map had been taken. The map, and whatever it may or may not lead to, appeared to be the sole motive for the burglary and, presumably, for Kilkarney's murder. For the past hour or so, there had been nothing to do but look out the front window at the rain.

193

"Well, it's four o'clock," Father said. "And I don't think we're going to get any more customers today. What say we close up and go home early? After these last two days, I say we deserve it."

"You won't get any argument from me," I said. "I'll even buy you an absinthe on the way home."

"I think the situation calls for it," he said with a nod and a smile. "Start turning off the lights, then, and I'll go check the back door. I want to take another look at that second lock I had installed."

I was making my way around the shop, turning off the gas to the lights, when the front door opened. My back was to the door and I couldn't see who entered. "You've just caught us in time," I said over my shoulder. "We were getting ready to leave." There was no response from whoever it was and I turned around and saw a cloaked and hooded figure, dripping wet, standing just inside the door. It was too dim in the shop to see the shadowed face. "Is there something I can help you with?"

Pale hands reached up and pulled back the hood. It was Carlotta Kilkarney. "Yes, Mr. Theriot, if you are willing, I do need your help."

* * *

We closed up the shop, drew the shades, and turned off all the lights except for the one over my drawing table. Carlotta sat at the table, her dark eyes red and swollen from tears and lack of sleep.

"I can only imagine what you two must think of us," she said in a strained voice. "But I swear to you before God, Papà was only trying to right a wrong he committed many years ago."

"Here is your tea, Miss Kilkarney," Father said, setting a cup and saucer in front of her. "It's not fresh, I'm afraid, but it is warm."

"Thank you, sir." Her hands trembled as she lifted the cup to her lips.

194

Her face was noticeably paler than when I had seen her yesterday.

"When did you last eat?" I asked.

"I'm fine, thank you, the tea will help. I must explain. I owe you that much." She set the cup down and took in a breath. "I'm afraid the tale starts a long time ago. My father was an airman, a navigator. He learned the craft as a young officer in the Royal Navy. He didn't stay long in the Queen's service, though, and when he left he came here, to New Orleans, to work the Caribbean trade routes. After he was here a few years he heard that the Mexican government was offering good wages for experienced airmen, especially navigators. They were charting air routes to their inland towns and villages."

"Yes, I remember that," Father said. "As a matter of fact, we keep several of those maps in our stock."

Papà was assigned to a small airboat with two other men, Connor, the boat captain, and Hacker, the engineer. They worked to chart the Yucatan Peninsula. One day, while they were making a survey flight, they passed over the top of a crumbling stone structure that had been nearly overtaken by the jungle. They had all heard tales of fabulous wealth hidden by the ancient Indians of the region in their tombs and temples. Several local officials involved in the survey effort had already gotten rich plundering the holy places of their ancestors.

"In the Yucatan that would have been the Mayan Indians, Father offered. "You remember, Paul, an exhibit of their art was on display for a while at the library. Sorry for the interruption, Miss Kilkarney, please continue."

"By mutual consent, they did not report the position of the temple. Instead, they went later on their own to investigate. What they found exceeded

195

their wildest dreams; enough gold and jewels to make a dozen men wealthy for a lifetime. They loaded everything they could find onto the airboat and fled to Cuba. But their luck turned bad before they got there. A storm blew them off course and brought the airboat down in the mountains near the coast. Hacker was severely injured in the crash. Papà and Connor made a litter and carried Hacker to the coast where they built a fire. A fishing boat saw the smoke and brought them to a nearby village. Papà and Connor returned later to the crash site, took what treasure they could carry, and hid the rest in a cave some distance from the wreck."

"Is that what your father's map shows then, the place where he and Connor hid the Mayan gold?" I asked.

"Yes. Hacker's injuries required him to be hospitalized for a while in Havana. Papà made the map while they were there. Once Hacker had recovered sufficiently, they split the treasure they had and went their separate ways, each with enough to be rich for the rest of their lives. Papà traveled through Europe and met my mother while she and her family were on holiday at Lake Como. They married and settled in Milan. But bad luck continued to plague the three of them. Connor was killed in Philadelphia when the boiler of the steam taxi he was riding in exploded. Mamma died a few years later, when I was six." Fresh tears started down her cheeks and she paused.

"I'm sorry," I said. "May I get you something else to drink?"

"No, but thank you, sir." She wiped the tears away and continued. "Hacker lost most of his wealth through high living and bad investments. And when his funds started to run short he came to Papà. Hacker wanted Papà to go with him to Cuba for the rest of the treasure. Mamma had just died the year before and Papà wanted nothing more to do with it. He gave Hacker money and asked him to go away. And every few years thereafter Hacker would return, each time more insistent than the last. He wanted the rest of the treasure."

"Why didn't your father just give Hacker the map and be done with it?" I asked.

"His conscience wouldn't allow it. Papà came to see the treasure as a curse, the cause of Mamma's death, the cause of all of their troubles. He knew they had done wrong in taking it and thought it was best left alone. Until last month that is, when Hacker came to see him again. Hacker was vocally abusive and made veiled threats against me if Papà didn't help him. Papà knew then that the only way to be free of Hacker and the treasure's influence was to return it to Mexico where it belonged. But he needed a ruse to separate himself from Hacker and buy time to get to the treasure first."

"So he did intend for the map to be stolen," I said.

"Yes," said Carlotta, lowering her eyes. "Papà told me he had taken some precautions when he made the map. He knew that if he could get Hacker to try to follow the map on his own, it would buy him the time he needed to get to the treasure first. He pretended to agree to Hacker's demands. He told Hacker the truth, the map was in a safety deposit box in New Orleans. Papà told Hacker to go to Havana. Papà would get the map and meet Hacker there."

"Knowing that Hacker would be suspicious and follow him to New Orleans," I said.

"Precisely. Once he was sure that Hacker was here and following us, Papà went to the bank to get the map and carried it in plain sight directly to your shop. By that time Hacker was convinced that Papà was planning to deceive him. Believing he was disrupting Papà's plans, Hacker broke into your shop to secure the map for himself."

197

"I have to admit it, your father's plan was clever," I said sincerely.

Carlotta smiled sadly. "Not clever enough, as it turned out. I don't think it ever occurred to Papà that Hacker would delay getting to the treasure long enough to murder him."

"Your father arranged to have us generously compensated for the damage to the shop," Father said. "We thank both of you for that. Paul and I are deeply sorry for your father's death and for your loss."

Carlotta smiled and nodded her thanks. There were no more tears, but her face was still dreadfully pale.

"I'm sure Paul will be happy to walk you to the police station, so you can tell them what you've told us."

"Thank you for kindness, sir, but I have no intention of going to the police," Carlotta said.

"But ... but you must. You must tell them about the man who killed your father. How else can justice be done?" Father asked what he probably thought was a rhetorical question.

"By fulfilling my father's wish; by beating Hacker to the treasure and returning the remainder of the Mayan gold to Mexico."

"My dear, you can't be serious," Father said.

"I assure you, sir, I am."

"You should take this to the police, or to the Mexican consulate. They can arrange to have the treasure found and returned," Father persisted.

"No." Carlotta was adamant. "Going through the authorities will take too long. Papà's map won't fool Hacker indefinitely. I have to get to the treasure before he does."

"What was the rest of your father's plan?" I asked.

"Paul, I really don't . . ." Father began to admonish.

"We were going to Key West. Papà had contacts there from his days in the Caribbean trade. Contacts I do not have. That is why I've come to you. I need your help to hire an airship and a reliable crew."

Father tried again to reason with Carlotta. "Now, Miss Kilkarney, realistically . . ."

"That's going to cost money; a lot of upfront money," I said.

"There, you see," Father said, a tone of finality in his voice.

"Before we left Milan, Papà sold our home and most of his business interests to finance this trip. I have that money. And I also have this." Carlotta reached behind her neck and unfastened a gold chain. She extracted a medallion from under her dress and laid it on the table. It was an exquisitely worked golden disk, incised with Mayan glyphs and set in the center with a large, uncut emerald. "It's the last intact piece from my father's share of the treasure. He gave it to my mother when they married."

My father leaned closer to examine the glittering disk. He was awestruck. "It's beautiful. I've never seen anything like it."

"Sebastian Vasquez is in town," I said. "He's about as honest a captain as you'll find anywhere. He should be somewhere in the Swamp."

"True," Father said. "But he'll take some convincing. My apologies, miss, but Capt. Vasquez is a practical man. Your tale may seem a bit, well, fanciful to him."

"Not if I go," I countered.

"Well, of course, you should," Father agreed. "You can't expect this young lady to go into a sordid district like the Swamp."

"I assure you, I am no shrinking violet," Carlotta said.

"No, Father, I mean go with her to recover and return the treasure."

It was a toss-up between them as to who was more surprised by my

199

statement.

"I cannot ask you to do that, Mr. Theriot," Carlotta said, but her eyes told me she hoped I would.

"You won't need to ask. I'm volunteering my services."

I glanced to Father and he glared at me for a long moment before he relented and laughed. "Yes, of course. For a lost Mayan treasure and a beautiful girl, if I were thirty years younger I'd probably go myself."

"I will never be able to thank you enough, either of you. I will pay you for your trouble, of course, Mr. Theriot."

"I'm sure you'll be more than fair," I said. Then looking over her nice clothes and fine jewelry, I added, "But Father does make a good point about the Swamp. A lady such as you would attract far too much unwanted attention. It'll be better if I go in alone and arrange a later meeting with Vasquez somewhere else."

Carlotta, however, was not going to be put off that easily. She thought for a few seconds and then asked, "Can you tell me where I can find a secondhand clothing shop?"

* * *

The transformation Carlotta affected was truly amazing; I would not have known her as the same woman. She had bought a faded, yellow, low-necked gown that she wore off her shoulders. Over this she draped a black, fringed shawl with a yellow, red, and green floral pattern. Her hair was worn up, but loose, held in place by a large gold-painted comb decorated with pieces of cut glass. She complimented her ensemble with an artful over-application of cheap makeup. With my old airman's jacket, worn dungarees, and cloth cap, we looked like so many other flyers, sailors, and boatmen out for a prowl though the Swamp with their favorite doxies.

200

Located at the back of town, the Swamp was a six-block stretch of shacks and shanties filled with saloons, flophouses, dance halls, and brothels. Although you could always find something going on in the Swamp, things really didn't start rolling until well after sunset. And by midnight it was positively roaring. I fully intended to have Carlotta, and me, out of there well before then. We had been to two places already and although I hadn't yet seen Vasquez, or any of his usual crew, I had seen acquaintances that had.

I had convinced Carlotta to get something to eat at our first stop and, once started, she had shown a good appetite. Having some food in her stomach, and doing something other than hiding from Hacker and the police, had done much to lift her spirits. I was sure that under that heavy makeup some color had returned to her cheeks. Our third stop that night was Mudcat Annie's. Annie always had a good piano player on staff and tonight was no exception. A rousing, piano-driven sing along of *Camptown Air Race* met us as we stepped through the front door.

"Goin' to fly all night, goin' to fly all day.

I bet my money on a hot air blimp,

And the wind done blowed it away."

I surveyed the crowded interior and almost immediately saw Victor, Vasquez's Senegalese first mate. Victor had served as sailing master on a Nantucket whaler before jumping to airships. No one knew wind and weather better than Victor.

"Paulo!" he yelled as he heard me call his name. He embraced me in a bear hug and then clamped his hands on my shoulders. "What are you doing here? Are you flying again?"

"Not exactly. I'll explain in a bit. Is Capt. Vasquez here?"

"Aye, he's out back shooting craps. Who's your friend?" he asked, noticing Carlotta at my elbow.

"Miss Kilkarney, this is Victor, an old shipmate from my flying days. Victor, this is Miss Carlotta Kilkarney."

"A pleasure, love," Victor said, extending a scarred and calloused hand.

If Carlotta was bothered by his ethnicity or familiarity, it didn't show. She took his hand and smiled. "Nice to meet you, sir."

"Can you tell the captain I want to talk to him? It's important."

"Sure, he's probably losing anyway. Until later, miss."

I led Carlotta over to an empty table near a corner and ordered us each a beer. When I sat down I saw that she was looking at me thoughtfully.

"What is it?" I asked.

"I'm sorry, it's just . . . well, you're different than what I had first imagined. When you came to the hotel you seemed . . ."

"Awkward?"

She smiled. "No . . . clerkish, I suppose. But you're very much at home here, among these people — airmen and sailors."

"Well, this was my life for a few years. But it's not home."

"Do you miss it?"

"Sometimes. When the moon is full, the sky is clear, and there's a fair breeze out to sea. Maybe that's why I was so quick to offer to come along."

"Why did you leave the air?"

"I made a promise to my father to return and help with the shop. And I realized that this was not the life for a man who one day wanted to settle down in one spot. I guess the clerkish part of me is a bit too strong."

Our beers arrived and we each took a healthy swallow.

"How well do you know Capt. Vasquez?" Carlotta asked.

"Pretty well, I'd say. I flew with him for about two and half years."

"And you trust him?"

I nodded. "He's got one or two minor vices, but he's scrupulously honest and very religious. You wouldn't know it to look at him now, but he was once a Jesuit seminarian."

"A seminarian with vices, how did the Jesuits let him get away?"

I smiled at her quip, pleased that she was showing a sense of humor. Before we could continue our conversation, however, a drunken boatman lurched into our table.

"Sorree," he slurred as he turned in our direction and then became entranced by the sight of Carlotta's cleavage. "I's has 'nough whiskey for tonight, darlin'," he drawled, wiping his mouth with the back of a dirty hand. "I thinks I'd like a nuzzle and some milk, now." He draped himself clumsily over Carlotta's shoulders and grabbed one of her breasts.

I pushed back my chair and stood up quickly. I had hoped to be in and out of the Swamp without attracting attention or trouble and I was wondering if I could get this rye-guzzler off Carlotta without getting into a fight—he was sure to have some friends close by. I need not have worried, however.

Carlotta pushed her face into the drunk's and hissed, "I'm no cow, you drunken sot, and if you don't leave go my teat, you'll spend the rest of your life a steer."

All the color drained from the man's face and as he slowly straightened up I saw that Carlotta had the barrel of a small revolver jammed into his crotch. The boatman turned unsteadily and staggered away as fast as he could. I was impressed.

"So, Miss Kilkarney," I asked as I sat back down. "Where did you learn that kind of language?"

Carlotta returned the revolver to her lap and shrugged her bare shoulders. "Romance novels."

Her response struck me as one of the funniest things I'd ever heard and I laughed wholeheartedly, with Carlotta joining in. We were still laughing when Vasquez, glass of wine in hand, swaggered up to our table. Portuguese by birth, Vasquez, with his shaven head, large mustache, gold earring, and tattooed arms, looked more like a Barbary pirate than a merchant captain.

"Paulo, why is it so long since I've seen you, eh? I'm hurt. You forget our old captain until you need him."

I ignored his jibes and rose to embrace my old friend. "It's good to see you, too, Seb."

"Paulo broke my heart when he left my crew," Vasquez said to Carlotta as he took a seat at the table. "I've never had a better navigator."

"Miss Kilkarney, this is Capt. Sebastian Vasquez. Capt. Vasquez, may I present Miss Carlotta Kilkarney."

"Well, my friend, your taste in women has certainly changed, and for the better I'd say." Vasquez leaned closer to Carlotta, as if to speak to her in confidence. "You should see the women he usually goes with — mousey, little frilly types who want to be escorted to tea parties and the opera." He made a face as if smelling something sour.

"*La donna è mobile*," commented Carlotta in Italian, a playful look in her eyes.

"Well, there's certainly nothing mousey about Miss Kilkarney," I stated. "And I should warn you, Captain, there's more to her than meets the eye."

"I don't know, Paulo," Vasquez said. "I can't see how there could be

204

much more."

"There's always more to a woman than what you can see, Captain," Carlotta countered.

Vasquez sighed and nodded his head. "Aye, and that's the part that probably gets me in trouble."

"Well, Captain, the lady is here to offer you yet another chance to get in trouble," I said.

"Oh?" Vasquez raised his eyebrows.

Carlotta leaned forward, lowered her voice, and raised the intensity of her tone. "Capt. Vasquez, thirty years ago three men stole a king's ransom in cursed Mayan gold and jewels. Two of those men are now dead. One of the dead men was my father. He was murdered yesterday by the third thief over a map to the treasure. I intend to get to the treasure first and return it to its rightful owners—the people of Mexico. I will pay you well, Captain, and in advance, for your help in righting this wrong, lifting the gold's curse on my family, and cheating my father's murderer of the spoils of his crimes."

Vasquez gave me a dubious look. Then Carlotta placed her hand, palm down, on top the table. She lifted her hand only long enough to give Vasquez a brief glimpse of the uncut emerald at the center of a glittering, golden disk.

Eyes wide, Vasquez whistled out a breath. *"Mãe de Deus."*

* * *

Vasquez's airship, *A Senhora*, was moored across the Mississippi River at the Algiers Depot. A 350-ton air schooner, *A Senhora* was built to standard airship design. She featured a ship's hull suspended beneath a large, blimp-shaped, hydrogen-filled airbag. A marine steam engine installed below deck supplied power for the schooner's multi-bladed propeller.

205

I brought Carlotta to the depot early on our day of our departure to stow our gear and help get her settled onboard. She was traveling light, just what she had on—a white blouse, khaki jodhpurs, and high lace-up boots—some personal items, a jacket, and a change of clothes. The female members of the crew had a separate area under the foredeck to hang their hammocks. Carlotta would be staying there—*A Senhora* had only the captain's cabin and Vasquez didn't give it up for anyone. She didn't seem to mind at all; though, I'd be willing to bet she had never before slept in such cramped and Spartan accommodations.

I knew most of the crew from my flying days and I introduced them to Carlotta as I gave her a tour of the ship. She extended her hand and had a pleasant word or two for each, eliciting smiles from even the surliest. As I brought Carlotta aft to see the helm station I saw another of my former shipmates near the airship's wheel. Maria-Teresa was a Yucatec Indian from the Central American Highlands. The Yucatec were descendants of the Maya and Maria-Teresa had the classic facial features depicted in their art.

"Miss Kilkarney, this is Maria-Teresa. Besides being a first class hand at the helm, Maria-Teresa is the ship's interpreter. I don't believe there's a language spoken around the Caribbean—European or Indian—that Maria-Teresa can't make herself understood in."

"I have an interest in languages, as well," Carlotta said as she took Maria-Teresa's hand. "Do you know any Italian?"

The question surprised Maria-Teresa. "No, senorita, I don't."

"I'd be happy to teach you some, if you'd like. And I'd like you to tell me something of the Indian languages you know."

"Yes, senorita, I'd like that very much, thank you."

Carlotta smiled. *"Sì, signorina, mi piacerebbe molto, grazie."*

206

"Was that what I just said, in Italian?" Maria-Teresa asked with an uncertain smile.

"*Sì, signorina, in Italiano.*"

"It sounds a lot like Spanish." Maria-Teresa beamed.

Carlotta laughed, then said in Spanish, "*Muy bien, señorita, el Italiano es muy parecido a Español. Vas a aprender en muy poco tiempo.*"

Carlotta seemed to have a way with people, and I was genuinely pleased she was getting on so well. But I was also beginning to see I was not going to have as much of Carlotta's time on this voyage as I had hoped.

* * *

We were one day out from Cuba and making good time. Carlotta, Vasquez, Victor, and I stood around a table in Vasquez's cabin. We studied a topographical map of the island on which I had marked from memory the location of the Maltese cross and had written down the riddle.

"'Twixt the peaks' refers to the spot where their airboat crashed. Papà told me they had gone down in a hollow on a mountainside south of two peaks," Carlotta said.

Vasquez put his finger on the map at a point where the topographical contours indicated two mountain peaks, just north of the Maltese cross. "The cross probably marks the crash site then, and not the location of the treasure."

"Then the rest of the riddle must refer to where the remaining treasure is hidden," said Carlotta.

"Had you ever seen your father's map?" I asked.

"No, I didn't even know it existed until recently."

"'Score the rod half water half rum,'" Vasquez read, and then shrugged his shoulders. "Mark a stick and mix a drink?"

"Well, a rod is a measure of distance," I ventured. "It equals five and

207

a half yards. And a score is twenty. Twenty times five and a half would equal one hundred and ten yards. That could be a relevant distance."

"The distance from the wreck?" asked Vasquez.

"That would make sense," Carlotta said. "We would just need a direction."

"'Half water half rum' — any ideas how that relates to a direction?" Vasquez asked.

"It could refer to a landmark," Victor suggested. "A tree or a rock formation."

"Maybe, but we could only tell that when we got on the ground," I said. "Half water and half rum, isn't that the mixture for British sailor's and airman's grog? Miss Kilkarney, you said your father had been in the Royal Navy. Did he ever mention anything about rum or grog that might apply?"

"No, not that I can think of," Carlotta replied.

"We could ask Limey Bob. He served on Royal airships for years," offered Victor.

"Just as well, call him in," Vasquez said.

It didn't take but a few minutes for Victor to bring Limey Bob, the ship's cook, into Vasquez's cabin.

"Bob, can you think of anything about British airman's grog that might have anything at all to do with a direction of any kind?" Vasquez asked.

Limey Bob stared down at the deck, rubbing his whiskered chin, and scrunching up his face while the four of us looked on expectantly. "No, Cap'n," he finally said. "Can't rightly say that I do."

"Well, it was worth a try," Vasquez said. "Thanks for your time, Limey."

"Not a problem, sir. G'evening, miss, gen'lemen." Limey Bob nodded to all present and headed for the door. He stopped just as he opened it and turned. "You was just askin' 'bout the common airmen and not the officers, wasn't you, Cap'n?"

Vasquez crooked his index finger and beckoned Limey Bob back to the table. "As long as you're here, Limey, why don't you tell us about the officers' grog?"

"Well, sir, the common airmen gets their grog only one way, you see, half rum and half water. The officers, now, they gets their choice. They can have their rum neat or with as much or as little water as they wants. I've known some officers, me being in the mess all those years and all, that called for their grog by compass points." He had all of our attention with that statement. "North is all rum, you see, and west is all water. So, an officer callin' for a course of due north would want his grog all rum and no water. 'Course, no one would take their grog all water, but some would call for west-north-west; that would be two-thirds water and one-third rum, you see. And so forth."

"So, half water and half rum would be ..." prompted Vasquez.

"Oh well, Cap'n, sir, that would be northwest, it would."

* * *

Thirty years of sun, rain, and wind had weathered the wreck of the old airboat until it was almost indistinguishable from the landscape. It had taken us the better part of a day to find it from the air. Vasquez brought *A Senhora* low over the wreck and Carlotta and I, along with Victor and Maria-Teresa, went over the side.

The area around the wreck was heavily overgrown with brush, vines, and stunted trees. Using a compass I led the way from the remains of the airboat along a rise up the mountainside. We hacked our way through the thick vegetation with cutlasses as we went. Vasquez gained altitude above us and

209

drifted slowly to the northwest, keeping tabs on us and maintaining a sharp lookout for any sign of Hacker.

Even though we didn't have very far to go, our progress was slow. It seemed we spent a minute slashing at vines for every few feet we traveled. The air was humid and filled with buzzing, stinging insects and the heavy growth shielded us from the sea breeze. By the time Victor called out that we had traveled one hundred and ten yards, we were soaked with sweat, covered with insect bites, and, except for Maria-Teresa, sucking in air like bellows.

"We only have a few hours before sunset," Victor said between deep breaths. "We need to spread out and start looking."

"Be careful where you walk," Maria-Teresa warned. "The cave mouth could be under our feet."

Several rocky outcroppings, all overgrown with vines, encircled us. And until an hour before sunset we poked and prodded, slashed at vines and swatted at bugs, swore and cursed, and found no signs of a cave. A pistol shot sounded from *A Senhora*.

"That's our signal," Victor said. "We need to go back to the wreck to be picked up before it gets too dark. Sorry, Miss Kilkarney, we'll have come back tomorrow."

"No," said Maria-Teresa. "Wave them off. We'll find the cave at dusk."

Victor rolled his eyes. "Maria-Teresa, we haven't been able to find the cave in the daylight, how are we going to find it when the sun goes down?"

"We just have to wait for them," she said.

"You're not making sense," said Victor. "Wait for who?"

"The bats."

* * *

210

At dusk, just as Maria-Teresa had said, the bats began to leave the cave. She had spread us out among the outcroppings and I was nearest the cave mouth when the bats took flight. I called to the others and made my way closer, marking the location by sight as a steady stream of the winged mammals flew off to feed on the bugs that had fed on us all day. Moving forward carefully by lantern light after the last bat had winged into the night, we found the entrance to the cave behind a thick cover of vines.

More familiar with this type terrain than any of the rest of us, Maria-Teresa led the way in with Carlotta following close behind. Victor and I brought up the rear.

The floor of the cave sloped down sharply from the entrance. Maria-Teresa was surefooted and we followed in her footsteps as we made our way into the darkness. After the heat and humidity outside, the cool air of the cavern felt good, but the stench of guano and urine from the bats made it far from pleasant.

After thirty feet or so, the downward slope became more gradual and the narrow passage broadened out into a large, circular chamber. Our bulls-eye lanterns cast eerie shadows on the cavern's irregular, multi-hued walls and stalagmite-studded floor. The sound of dripping water echoed hollowly in the distance. Prompted by our presence the last of the bats left their perches on the lofty ceiling. They whirled above our heads before flying off into the night.

"Watch out for spiders," Maria-Teresa cautioned.

"Wouldn't the bats have eaten them?" asked Victor.

"No," she answered. "These spiders eat bats."

"Oh," Victor said. He turned to me and added, "Sorry I asked."

Maria-Teresa led us clockwise around the chamber. We searched along the walls and across those areas of the cave floor relatively free of the bats' droppings. There were a few side passages off the main chamber and we searched those as far back as it appeared safe; or as far as reasonable for men carrying gold to have traveled.

After nearly four hours of searching, and having nearly completed our circuit around the central chamber, we had found no trace of the Mayan gold. I caught a brief glimpse of Carlotta's face in the lantern light. Her face was dirty and still streaked from the sweat of our trek up the side of the mountain. I saw a trace of anxiety in Carlotta's eyes; we were running out of cave to search.

Our order of march had become reversed as we made our way back to the cave's entrance. Victor led the way, followed by me, then Carlotta and Maria-Teresa.

"I don't know, Paulo, maybe there's another cave in the area," Victor said over his shoulder as we neared the spot where we had started our search. "Or, another entrance to this cave. Maria-Teresa, what do you think?"

When Maria-Teresa didn't answer Victor and I stopped and looked behind us. Maria-Teresa and Carlotta were standing some ways back. Maria-Teresa was shining the beam of her lantern up toward the cavern's ceiling.

Victor and I walked back to join the women.

"What is it?" I heard Carlotta ask.

Maria-Teresa used the beam of her lantern to point out a pile of rocks that lay in an alcove against the wall. "Those rocks didn't fall from the ceiling," she said. "They were placed there."

Victor was closest; he walked over and squatted down to examine the pile. We followed and saw him reach out and pull at something protruding from between two chunks of stone. "There's oil cloth under the rocks," he said with a broad smile. "I think we may have found something."

Victor and I moved the rocks out of the way and Carlotta and Maria-Teresa pulled back a large sheet of oil cloth. And there, underneath, spread out among the rotting remains of canvas bags, was the unmistakable glimmer of gold.

"Oh, my God," whispered Carlotta.

My heart pounded in my chest. Figurines of gold, cups of gold, disks of gold, beads of gold. And scattered among the gold were emeralds, rubies, and pieces of jade. What a man could do with all this wealth!

That unbidden, avaricious thought was driven from my head by the incongruous sound of weeping. Maria-Teresa dropped slowly to her knees. She reached out a trembling hand to reverently touch the exquisitely crafted, gold figurine of a seated woman with a jade, mosaic snake perched atop her head.

"She is Ixchel, our goddess of childbirth." Maria-Teresa turned tear-filled eyes to Carlotta. "Gracias, senorita, God will bless you for what you are doing."

* * *

A Senhora was gaining altitude for our flight over the mountains and our return to New Orleans. The afternoon sky was overcast. A light rain was falling. The treasure had been safely stowed onboard and everyone was in a jubilant mood. As we climbed higher the air temperature dropped. The crew were donning jackets, gloves, and scarves for the colder temperatures when we heard the shout we had been dreading.

"Ship ho!" cried the lookout.

"Damn me," Vasquez swore. "Where away?"

"Two points aft the starboard bow," the lookout answered. "Half a league out and coming fast, heading due west."

213

"Helm, turn us out to sea. Victor, I want full boiler pressure and full speed, now!"

"Aye, aye, Captain."

We hung on to railing and rigging as *A Senhora* heeled over hard to port. When we had settled on a course that would put us out to sea, we ran to the schooner's side.

"What ship is she?" Vasquez demanded.

"A sloop, sir," called the lookout.

"Good, we're bigger," said Vasquez.

"Captain, it's the *Retribution*," the lookout added.

"Blanchard's ship," Vasquez said, then spat over the side.

"Who's Blanchard?" Carlotta asked.

"A pirate, pure and simple, and good company for Hacker if they're together," I answered.

"Why are we heading out to sea?" asked Carlotta.

"A bit of strategy; if Hacker is with Blanchard, then they know about the treasure and they want it. The easiest way to take down an airship is by taking out the airbag. If we're over water when we go down, we'll likely capsize and sink, and they'll lose the treasure. To be sure of getting it, they'll have to get close enough to board us. We, however, can target their airbag. It gives us an advantage."

Vasquez had his spyglass trained on the *Retribution*. "She's turning to follow. Man the stern swivel guns. Victor, where's our speed?"

"Boiler's at full pressure, Captain. You'll have your steam presently."

Vasquez moved to the stern and Carlotta and I followed. Two crew members operated each swivel gun. Capable of firing one-inch-diameter lead spheres in a wide arc, swivel guns were mounted all along the ship's gunwales.

"Guns loaded with round shot and primed, Captain."

"Damn, she's fast," Vasquez hissed, peering through his spyglass at the steadily gaining airship. Under our feet we could feel the increase in vibration as the engineer throttled more steam to the piston. Our speed began to increase, but it would not be enough. The *Retribution* was gaining too fast. Eventually, we'd have to turn and fight.

"Get ready to fire both stern guns, let them know we intend to fight. Fire!" Vasquez ordered.

The two stern swivel guns fired, spitting flame and smoke into the drizzling gloom.

"Are those the largest guns we have?" Carlotta asked.

"Yes. All airships, no matter the size, are lighter than air. If we were to fire a full broadside of deck guns, like they do on surface ships, it'd set us swinging like a pendulum under the airbag."

"She's not slowing, Captain," the lookout called.

"Who's up there?" asked Vasquez. "Isaac? Isaac, get your ass down on the deck. You'll be the first one killed up there in the crow's nest." Vasquez turned to address Carlotta and me, "There's no doubt, they're after the treasure." He then addressed his gunners. "Reload the stern guns. Commence firing at their airbag as soon as they're in range."

"Aye, Captain."

"Victor, check all guns — port, starboard, and bow — make sure they're loaded with round shot and primed; and I want grapeshot ready when they're close enough to try to grapple."

"Aye, aye, captain."

With each passing second Blanchard's *Retribution* was getting closer. The pirate sloop's hull was painted black, trimmed in red, and the airbag above it was its opposite, red with black trim.

"Limey Bob, open up the armory — pistols, pikes, and cutlasses for all. Can you shoot, Miss Kilkarney?" Vasquez asked Carlotta.

"Aye, Captain, and handle a fencing sword," she replied.

"Limey, a pistol and a rapier for the lady," Vasquez said. Then he added with a smile to me, "She's a keeper, Paulo. If we live."

Our stern guns fired again, almost simultaneously with the *Retribution's* bow guns.

"Blanchard will be aiming for our propeller, to slow us down," I explained to Carlotta. I noticed she was tense, understandably so, and hanging on to the railing with a white-knuckled grip. I leaned on the railing next to her.

"These people are putting their lives in danger so I can fulfill my father's wish," she said. Her dark eyes were large and liquid. "I don't want anyone else to die. If we hand over the gold to the pirates, will they let us go?"

"Everyone on board understood the risks when they signed on," I told her. "And they all know what type of man Bloody Blanchard is; he'd as soon break his word as keep it. We have to see this through."

She turned her head to look at the fast-approaching *Retribution*. "If Hacker is aboard that airship, I will kill him."

Given the chance, I believed she would.

* * *

A Senhora and *Retribution* punctuated the darkening afternoon with periodic, concussive retorts of cannon fire that filled the cold, damp air with the smell of gunpowder. We had not been hit yet, but their shots were ranging closer. Assisted by Isaac, Limey Bob passed out revolvers, boarding pikes, and swords. He gave Carlotta and me each a Navy Colt revolver. I took a cutlass and Limey presented Carlotta with a rapier with a fancy, scrolled hand guard.

216

"Hope this suits you, miss, it belonged to one of the cap'n's ladies," Limey said. Then he shook his head sadly. "It near broke his heart the day she was hanged."

"Then, I hope to do it justice and return it to you bloodied," Carlotta said, testing the blade's balance.

"Aw, bless your heart, miss, I'm sure you'll do us proud," said Limey.

A sharp, metallic prang signaled a hit to *A Senhora's* propeller. The schooner started to shake violently and yaw to port. At least one blade had been bent, throwing the propeller out of balance.

"Victor, half speed! Helm, keep us straight! Gunners, man the port guns. Prepare to turn and fight."

The reduction in speed eased the airship's shaking, but meant the air pirates would soon be on us. "There's still a good chance we'll be able to fight them off, keep them from getting close enough to grapple," I told Carlotta.

"How much damage will their airbag take before their ship goes down?" she asked.

"*Retribution's* airbag will be double-walled and honeycombed. It may take a couple of dozen hits before she starts losing lift. Vasquez's gunners are good and Blanchard's airship will have to get within about thirty yards to be able to throw grappling hooks. Even with our damaged propeller we still have the advantage."

A glance back to the pirates' airship, though, and I wasn't feeling so confident. Her deck was jammed with as villainous a crew as one would hope never to see, and they appeared to outnumber us three to one. Seeing our airship was wounded and slowing, they were working themselves up into a murderous frenzy. If they were able to grapple, we'd be in for a desperate hand-to-hand fight.

217

"Helm, hard over. Show them our port side," Vasquez bellowed. "Victor, fire as soon as the guns will bear."

A Senhora heeled over smartly and Victor had each swivel gun fire in sequence as soon as the *Retribution* was within their fields of fire. As soon as a gun was fired, it was reloaded to fire again. The helm kept our port side to the pirates and the gunners maintained a steady stream of round shot against the bow of their airbag. But the pirate airship kept coming on fast, right into the teeth of our guns.

Then, at about eighty yards out, the *Retribution* turned suddenly to port and ran parallel to our course. Three bright flashes appeared on the sloop's deck and streaked towards us.

"What the hell . . ." Vasquez began.

"They're rockets," Victor said in disbelief.

We watched in stunned amazement as the rockets swiftly crossed the distance between our two airships. One flew across our bow, and one, by the sound it made, deflected off our keel, but the third hit us squarely in the hull, rocking *A Senhora* to starboard. I had expected the rocket to explode, but it didn't. I looked over the side to see the rocket, sputtering out, firmly imbedded in our airship's side. The rocket had been fitted with a harpoon head and a thin metal line that extended back to *Retribution*. The slack went out of the metal line and *A Senhora* lurched toward the air pirates' vessel. We had been harpooned like a whale and were now being reeled in like a fish.

"Load the port guns with grapeshot. Fire at those damned sons of bitches as soon as they're in range. Limey Bob, take Isaac below and get that blasted rocket out of my lady's side. I'll skin that bastard Blanchard alive. Victor, drop the boarding nets. All hands, prepare to repel boarders."

Like most airships, *A Senhora* was built with a metal frame about twelve feet above the deck for the airbag to rest on when it's deflated. Vasquez had cargo nets fitted and rolled to the tops of the frames along both sides of the airship. Victor and the crew lowered the nets on our port side to provide a barrier to the inevitable boarders. They'd have to climb over or hack their way through to get to our deck. And while they were doing that we'd be able to dispatch a lot of them with our pistols and sword points.

The crew of the *A Senhora* gathered their weapons and assembled along the port-side railing. They shook weapons and fists at the pirates and returned our opponents' bloody taunts. Blanchard's pirates took some potshots at our crew and gunners. Vasquez ordered everyone to take shelter behind the gunwales. Gunners from both airships opened fire. Grapeshot peppered *A Senhora*'s sides and whizzed over our heads. One of our gunners was hit, a piece of grapeshot tearing a bloody gouge in her upper arm; we had taken our first casualty. I looked to Carlotta. She was afraid — just as I was — but steady as a rock.

As the range closed, the *Retribution* fired another harpoon rocket into our airship's hull. "God damn you, Blanchard," Vasquez raged. "I'll have your skull for an ale mug."

I risked a glimpse over the top of the gunwale. The distance between the airships was decreasing rapidly. I also saw pirates twirling smoldering slings over their heads. I knew what that meant and yelled out a warning. "Grenades!"

The nets deflected most of the grenades. They detonated harmlessly over the side. Two, however, made it over the top of the net and several of our crew were hit with shrapnel when the grenades exploded. The air pirates opened up on us with volleys of pistol shots and curses.

"Keep your heads down," Victor yelled above the din. "Wait until they're on the nets."

I made eye contact with Carlotta. Any optimistic words of encouragement would have sounded hollow just then, so I opted for some practical advice. "When you shoot, aim for the center of the torso. When you lunge, go for the belly."

It seemed she wanted to say something, but either couldn't think of the right words, or couldn't say them. She nodded and the corners of her mouth twitched up in a brief, uncertain smile.

Pirates, whether they're on the sea or in the air, aren't usually much on tactical finesse. They rely mostly on intimidation and sheer numbers to overcome their opponents. Blanchard's crew — may God have mercy on their souls, because I certainly didn't spare them any — was no exception. As soon as the airships were close enough, they began jumping across, scrambling for handholds on the nets and the sides of *A Senhora*. A few slipped and fell screaming to their deaths.

"Now, my hardies! Now, my bully boys!" Victor bellowed. "Up and at 'em. Send them back to the devils that spawned them."

Carlotta and I stood up. She ducked away from a pirate who reached for her through the netting. Carlotta turned, cocked the hammer of her pistol, and shot the man in the chest. She stared wide-eyed as he gurgled up blood and fought for grip on the net before falling away. I grabbed her and pulled her behind me.

"They're still firing from their airship. Keep a pirate between you and their ship. Kill that one and move on to the next, but keep moving."

The crew of *A Senhora* shot with pistols and stabbed and slashed with pikes and swords. I thrust my cutlass into one pirate and hacked off the hand of another. Across the way on the *Retribution*, I could see Blanchard —

220

tall, dark, and cadaverous, and wearing his signature red headscarf — exhorting his bloody-minded crew to press the attack.

Many pirates died on the net, but eventually they gained a foothold on our deck near the bow. I started using my revolver then, dropping four pirates with as many shots. We held them there for a while, but their numbers began to tell. Too many of *A Senhora's* crew lay wounded and bleeding on our deck.

"Fall back," I heard Vasquez shout. "Stay together, but fall back. Keep them in front of us."

Blanchard had jumped across to *A Senhora's* deck and was screaming in the midst of his crew. "Cut 'em down, cut 'em all down and the treasure will be ours. Chop 'em into bloody chum."

I lost track of Carlotta in the melee. She wasn't in front of me and I was hoping to God she was somewhere in back. I put myself in the front rank, shoulder to shoulder with Vasquez and Victor, as we fought and fell back, step by step, toward the stern.

Then *A Senhora* shifted. Her bow drifted away and slightly up from the *Retribution* and her stern dropped and settled closer to the pirates' airship. The movement could have been caused by our retreat toward the stern, or it could indicate that Limey and Isaac had freed our airship from one of the harpoon rockets. They would have to get the second one out a lot quicker if we were to stand any chance of survival.

The sudden movement of *A Senhora* brought a halt to the fighting as both sides strove to maintain their balance on the unsteady deck. During the lull I located Carlotta off to my right. She was providing cover while Maria-Teresa helped a wounded shipmate to the rear of our line. Blood ran down one side of Carlotta's face from a wound to her scalp, but she held the bloody point of the rapier steady out in front of her, sword arm extended, elbow and knees flexed.

I handed my pistol to Vasquez. "There're two shots left. Take out Blanchard if you get the chance."

Vasquez nodded. "Thank you, my friend." He then directed the crew to fall back further. *A Senhora* narrowed toward the stern, our defensive line could stand a bit closer and deeper.

For the moment at least, the pirates didn't seem inclined to press the attack. They had already lost far more crew members than they had expected. I used the extra time and space to move toward Carlotta. As I did, I heard one of the pirates call out. "There you are, you Black Irish bitch. I should have done for you in Milan when I had the chance."

So, that was Hacker. The bushy beard must have been a disguise; the man who taunted her had only a scraggly mustache adorning his weaselly face.

"Take your chance now, Hacker, if you've the balls for it," Carlotta hurled back at him.

The pirates around Hacker found Carlotta's romance-novel vocabulary as amusing as I did and started laughing. Hacker, however, failed to see the humor in Carlotta's comeback. He turned bright red and dug a pistol out of his belt. Carlotta was too far away to use her sword and Hacker was too close to miss her. And I had just handed my revolver to Vasquez!

More out of desperation than any preformed idea, I reared back and hurled my cutlass. It spun like a steam-powered circular saw and struck Hacker on the forearm. He howled bloody murder and the pistol fell from his hand. The pirates thought that was even funnier.

"Thank you," Carlotta said as I came up beside her. "And thank you for not killing him."

"This little fandango has lasted long enough," Blanchard called out, making sure everyone on board could hear him. "A double . . . no, a triple share of the treasure for any man, or woman, who brings me Vasquez's head!"

Blanchard knew how to motivate his crew. They surged forward with renewed, murderous vigor. Blanchard also knew how to keep himself out of harm's way. He kept moving and stayed just far enough back in his crew's ranks as they would allow him to get away with. Vasquez took a shot at Blanchard, but hit one of the pirates as they rushed forward.

Our front rank nearly collapsed under the ferocious onslaught. And without a weapon other than my airman's knife, I had to move behind Carlotta. She covered for me while I cast about desperately for anything I could use as a weapon.

"Here, Paulo, my cutlass." It was Victor. He looked ghastly. One of his ears had been nearly slashed off and he was holding a wad of cloth against a gaping wound in his side.

I got down on one knee. Taking the cutlass from his bloody fingers, I said, "Okay, mate, but only until you get your breath back."

He smiled weakly and closed his eyes.

I turned back to the fight in time to see Maria-Teresa go down, bleeding from a deep gash to her face, and a burly pirate drawing back his sword for a lunge to finish her off. Carlotta jumped in from the side, straddled Maria-Teresa, and parried the lunge. Then in less time than it takes to blink an eye, she disengaged the blade of her rapier and drove its point though the man's throat.

As the pirate staggered back, blood spraying in time to the beating of his heart, I jumped forward into the gap he had left. Hacking and slashing right and left, I drove two pirates back with fresh wounds, then turned and helped Carlotta drag Maria-Teresa to relative safety at the stern post.

Our crewmates closed ranks behind us and we had a moment of respite. Carlotta clutched my arm. "I am so sorry," she said. I could see her eyes were filled with tears and I knew the tears were not for her. I didn't know if they were for me in particular, but I loved her for them, anyway. I leaned in and kissed her on the mouth, and she kissed back. I broke off reluctantly and looked into her large, dark eyes – the deepest, most expressive eyes I had ever seen. And the way the light from the stern lantern seemed to form a halo around her bloodied but beautiful face … I got the craziest, most impulsive idea.

"Well, Miss Kilkarney," I said with a smile. "If we're going to go down, let's all go down in flames."

The brass mounting for the stern lantern broke after a good, hard hit from my cutlass. I caught the lantern by part of the mounting as it fell away and taking three long strides, I flung the lit lantern up and outward in a soaring arch. The gracefully arcing lantern caught nearly everyone's attention. Standing frozen in place, they followed the lantern's comet-like path against the grey sky, until it shattered in a pool of flame on the deck of the *Retribution*.

"Paulo, you magnificent bastard," Vasquez enthused. "Hey, Blanchard, what are you going to do now? Your airship is on fire."

"I'll eat your liver, that's what I'll do. You four, get back over there and put out that fire. And I'll roast you alive if my ship burns," Blanchard glowered. "For the rest of you, let's finish this. Half my share for the whore's son who threw that lantern."

And so, they set on us again. There were only about eight of us still standing against twenty or so air pirates. Two of them rushed Vasquez. He used his last bullet to save his life. Maria-Teresa was up on one elbow, holding

224

a bloody rag to the side of her face, and vehemently cursing in a mixture of Spanish and Yucatec. I had no idea where Victor was; I hoped he had been able to crawl somewhere out of the way. Carlotta and I fought shoulder to shoulder by the starboard rail. All of us were wounded to some extent, and fatigued. It was only sheer desperation that kept us going.

The fire burned aboard *Retribution* and Blanchard kept up a steady stream of curses against his crew, haranguing them blasphemously for their failure to kill us quickly. Hacker stood back from the fight, cradling his wounded arm, and probably waiting for the chance to swoop in and cut the throats of the injured. I knew Carlotta wanted to kill him and I would have liked to help her get the chance, but to break ranks then would only have hastened the demise of the rest of our crew. We had to wait and see how things played out. And play out they did.

A spitting, hissing sound came from the deck of the *Retribution*, along with a terrified cry. "The rockets! Cap'n Blanchard, the fire's got to the rockets."

For the third time that gloomy afternoon the fighting ceased. All eyes turned to *Retribution*. A bright red fountain of sparks erupted amidships and first one, then a second, and a third rocket skittered off to wreak havoc aboard the pirates' airship. The air pirates aboard *A Senhora* drifted away from us and watched horrified as the loose rockets spread fire and destruction across the sloop's deck.

Out of the corner of my eye I saw Carlotta move along the starboard rail. I knew where she was going and I followed. We passed pirates without them taking notice. Hacker had turned toward *Retribution* and Carlotta walked up behind him without being seen.

"Hacker," she said, her tone almost conversational. He started like a scared rabbit and his eyes went wide when he saw her so close. He fumbled with the pistol at his belt. She waited until he started to raise it before plunging twelve inches of steel into his belly. "For my father," she hissed and twisted the rapier in his guts.

Another sudden lurch of *A Senhora* jerked Hacker off Carlotta's blade. We were drifting away from the burning *Retribution*. Limey Bob and Isaac had succeeded in dislodging the second harpoon.

"Damn your eyes, Vasquez," Blanchard wailed. "It's your ship I'll have and your guts for a sword belt."

Carlotta and I were preparing to engage the air pirates from the flank when the forward hatch was flung open and Limey Bob and Isaac popped up, revolvers in hand. They immediately started blazing away. Bloody Blanchard was among the first to fall.

Vasquez led the charge from the stern, Carlotta and I attacked from starboard, and, once their pistols were empty, Limey Bob and Isaac laid into the pirates from the bow. Leaderless, surrounded, and with their airship sliding away in flames, it wasn't long before the remaining air pirates threw down their weapons and begged for quarter.

* * *

I don't think New Orleans had ever seen anything quite like the funeral Mass Carlotta had said for her father and *A Senhora's* crew members who had been killed in the battle with the *Retribution*. Considering the ferocity of the fight, the butcher's bill for our side had been relatively light. There were four coffins along the center aisle of the Cathedral, including the one holding Errol Kilkarney. Five of our crew mates were still recuperating in Charity Hospital. Victor was among them; the old whaler was just too hard to kill.

Carlotta had donated generously to the families of the slain crew

226

members and had spared no expense on the Mass. The archbishop himself presided over the service. There was an organist, a full choir, and as many candles and as much incense as the fire code would allow. Carlotta looked stunning in a black silk mourning dress with a veiled hat that, for the most part, hid the bandage wound around her head. Father and I sat with her in the front pew.

Quentin McCoy from the bank came, as well as a full delegation from the Mexican consulate, resplendent in full dress, military uniforms, and formal attire. All the walking wounded from *A Senhora* attended, of course, along with, it seemed, about half of the frequenters of the Swamp, wearing whatever finery or foppery they felt was appropriate. And to their credit, most of them were sober.

After the service Carlotta and I followed her father's coffin out to the street where four horse-drawn hearses waited. Three would head to St. Louis Cemetery. The one carrying Errol Kilkarney would go to the Gentilly Airship Terminal to the east of the city. In less than three hours Carlotta would be leaving to accompany her father home to Milan to be buried beside his wife.

Carlotta stayed near the steps of the Cathedral and graciously thanked everyone who had attended. When the Mexican consul appeared, Carlotta reached behind her neck and detached the chain holding the emerald adorned, golden disk. "Generalissimo Perez, here is the last piece. Thank you so much for allowing me to wear it today."

"A small favor, senorita, and one you richly deserve, especially after the trials you have endured. The government and people of Mexico will forever be grateful to you." The generalissimo kissed Carlotta's hand and shook mine. "There is also the matter of the bounty my government has offered for the pirate Blanchard; and if I am not mistaken at least four other

227

countries have bounties on him, as well."

"The bounties should go to Capt. Vasquez and his crew," I suggested. "With your permission, Generalissimo, I shall speak to him and direct him to contact you." Considering the amount of money Carlotta had paid him, and with multiple bounties for ridding the region of one of our most notorious air pirates, Vasquez and the crew had done well.

As the crew of *A Senhora* filed out, Carlotta raised her veil and together we shook hands, embraced, or kissed them as they passed. Maria-Teresa, her face stitched up and swollen purple, took Carlotta's hands and would have kissed them. Carlotta would have none of that, however; she pulled her hands away and the two women embraced like sisters.

Vasquez, his left arm in a sling, made a big show of doffing his plumed hat and bowing low before kissing Carlotta on both cheeks. "Miss Kilkarney, I know you are a lady, but I have seen that you have the heart of a brigand."

She shrugged her shoulders and smiled. "I am my parents' daughter, Captain."

"You will always have a berth on any airship I command."

Vasquez and I embraced, then he said, "Old friend, come find us in the Swamp tonight. We all need to get drunk together."

"I have a better idea," I responded. "Let's sneak a few bottles of wine into the hospital and we can all get drunk with Victor and the rest."

"I like that," Vasquez said smiling. "We can have good time. Until they kick us out."

"They won't kick us out if we bring a bottle or two for the orderlies, as well."

My father was the last one to come up. "I'll see to it that your father's coffin is properly and respectfully stowed onboard, Miss Kilkarney. There's no need for you and Paul to hurry."

"Thank you, Mr Theriot. I'm so sorry for all the trouble Papà and I have caused you."

"Oh no, my dear. I'm just grateful that you and Paul have returned relatively unscathed."

The hearses had pulled away. The crowd was following. Carlotta and I were alone.

"How is your leg?" she asked.

Along with a few cuts and bruises in various places, I had taken a sword point in the thigh during the last stage of the fight. I had a bandage wrapped around my leg and was walking with the aid of a cane. "It stiffed up a bit during the service. I think a bit of a walk will do it good."

There was a flower vendor at the opening of the alley between the Cathedral and the Cabildo. Carlotta bought a bouquet of mixed flowers. "Paul, hold them for me, please. A yellow one, I think," she said, selecting a flower and breaking off all but about four inches of the stem. She inserted the flower in the button hole of my lapel and smiled. "There, it matches the color of the dress I wore the first time you escorted out me for tea."

"I remember," I said. "A yellow dress, a floral shawl, and a pistol."

"A necessary accessory for the kind of places you bring me." She took back the bouquet and slipped her arm through mine. We walked toward Lafitte Square.

"What will you do now?" I asked. "I mean, after you've seen to your father's burial."

"I intend to sell off the rest of Papà's business interests and investments and give the money away. There's a pan-European charity for the widows and orphans of airmen and sailors, I think I'll donate the money to them."

I knew what that was about; she was getting rid of absolutely everything her father had gained from his share of the stolen treasure. "How will you live?"

"Mamma had some money of her own, from her family. It came to me when she died. That will last me a few years, if I'm careful." After a few paces she asked, "Paul, won't you, please, consider taking something for all the trouble I've caused you?"

"Thank you, but no. It would feel awkward taking money from you."

"Why? Because I'm a woman?"

"No, because I've fallen in love with you."

"Oh, Paul."

"I know you still have a lot to deal with, but I couldn't let you leave without saying something."

"No, you were right to say it. I've been struggling in my own mind to find the right words to express how I feel about you. I suppose it's been difficult because I truly do not know. I do love you, Paul, but right now the strongest feeling I have is gratitude for all you've done. Try as I might, I can't tell where my gratitude ends and my love for you begins. I'm sorry, Paul, but I'm afraid it may take me some time to sort it all out. But when I do, I promise, I will come to you in person and tell you how I feel. Will you wait for me?"

I stopped and turned to face her. "Yes, Carlotta, I'll wait," I answered. "But only for so long." I caressed her cheek and smiled. "Then I'll come to Milan and find you." I kissed Carlotta and felt her lips move softly against mine. We embraced and she whispered into my ear. "Thank you."

We continued the rest of the way in silence, through the entrance to the square, and on to the statue at the center. I indicated to Carlotta the spot at the back of Capt. Lafitte's statue where her father had died. The pedestal upon which the statue stood rested on a grassy mound encircled by a black, wrought iron fence. Carlotta knelt at the fence and placed the bouquet on the grass beyond the bars. With my injured leg I couldn't kneel or squat, so I stood beside her.

Carlotta reached up and took my hand. "You were here when he was shot."

"Yes," I said. "And I was with him when he died. He didn't suffer much, he went quickly. The last thing he did was say your name."

She lowered her head and I held her hand while she softly cried.

After a while, when her crying had ceased, she said, "He was a good man, a devoted husband, and a loving father. And that's the way I'll remember him." She paused, and then added, "Even though he had the poor grace to be shot beneath the Captain's ass."

She stood up, smiling through her tears.

"And here you are," she said, turning to me. Her eyes were still sad, but her smile was broadening. "Another airman, another navigator, another dashing adventurer trying to sweep another poor, young Italian girl off her feet."

"My dear," I said. "My broom isn't big enough to sweep you off your feet."

"Perhaps, you should let me be the judge of that," she said, and there was that playful gleam in her eyes again.

Her expression turned serious and, with her palm turned away from her, she spread the fingers of her right hand. "This ring has been in my mother's family for over three hundred years, passed down from parent to child. She gave it to me the night before she died. Mamma asked me to swear on the love I had for her to give the ring only to one of my own children, or to someone else in her family. So, this is not a gift." She took off the ring and held it out to me. "I want you to hold it for me, in trust, as my pledge to you that I will come back."

I had never seen anything like it before. It appeared to be made of thin gold wire, tightly woven around a smoky, red stone. I took her hand, kissed it, and pushed the ring into her palm. "That won't be necessary, Carlotta. Your promise is enough."

Arm in arm, we walked away from the center of the square toward the riverfront. Carlotta leaned against me and sighed contentedly.

"How much time do we have before the airship leaves?" she asked.

"About two and a half hours. That leaves us a little time. What would you like to do?"

"More than anything, Paul, I would just like to sit with you somewhere quiet. For as long as we possibly can."

I thought for a moment then squeezed her arm. "Then what would you say, my dear, to a long ride in a slow, closed carriage?"

END